An Open Mind

An Open Mind

a novel by Susan Sallis

Harper & Row, Publishers

New York, Hagerstown, San Francisco, London

An Open Mind
Copyright © 1978 by Susan Diana Sallis

FIRST EDITION

Library of Congress Cataloging in Publication Data
Sallis, Susan.
    An open mind.

    SUMMARY: Torn by conflicting loyalties and emotions
a teenage boy finally comes to terms with his father's
pending remarriage with the help of a spastic boy.
    [1. Fathers and sons—Fiction.   2. Physically
handicapped—Fiction.   3. Divorce—Fiction]   I. Title
PZ7.S15330p 1978   [Fic]   77-25678
ISBN 0-06-025162-X
ISBN 0-06-025163-8 lib. bdg.

1

You're supposed to start a story at the beginning, but I'm not sure where the beginning of mine really started, so I'll go straight into the bit where I went to see the teacher in charge of pastoral care. That was after I'd been caught smoking in the can when I should have been half killing myself in a rugby scrum.

She was sitting at one of the tile-topped coffee tables we made in woodwork, which was supposed to be a chattier setup than the usual desk and two chairs. Or even one chair for her, and me standing up nice and straight and respectful. She wasn't bad-looking, either. Strong black hair combed down past her shoulders, brown eyes, no makeup or nail varnish. What Mum calls a "sweater-and-skirt" type, but young with it. Her name was Miss Ruskin, and she did sex talks and held discussion groups in Comparative Religion as well as this pastoral-care bit.

She said, "Going through a bad patch lately, David, aren't you?"

That got me. It was supposed to cover not only a couple of recent cases of cheek to the teachers, plus the smoking incident, but the home background, too. I was supposed to start blabbing out my "personal difficulties" right away. Instead of which I clammed straight up as usual when I felt they were using the kid gloves on me. Humoring me. As if I was round the bend and didn't know about it. Perhaps that's how people feel in nuthouses and that's why they yell and carry on or just sit and look miserable.

She didn't wait too long in case the silence got awkward. She got hold of a bit of her hair and twisted it round her finger and said, "Want to talk about it? I could get hold of some coffee or Pepsi or something, if you like."

"No, thanks."

Sometimes my voice sounds like the electric saw in the woodwork room when it bites into some green wood. It starts off shrill and aggressive and then dies sullenly.

A couple of tiny muscles under her brown eyes contracted suddenly. She was annoyed and didn't want to show it. She didn't know whether I meant no to the Pepsi or to the chat or to both.

She decided to come to grips.

"Well. What's it all about then, David?"

There was a song somewhere started with those words, and I sang it in my head so I wouldn't have to think about her question.

It was so stupid, so crass. I'd been caught smoking in the boys' lavatories—that was the answer. But if it had been anyone else they'd have had the chat then and there, a quick detention, a couple of empty threats and straight out onto the field double quick. But I get sent to the teacher in charge of pastoral care.

She saw the silence building up again and she said,

"We understand you have difficulties, you know. We're not inhuman."

That was the trouble, they were too human. When she said "we," that meant a whole heap of people. There are sixty members of staff at our school and they've nearly all got yappy wives and kids. Very human. They must have had a field day when Dad and Mum eventually split up. It's a small town and Dad worked in the one and only engineering factory, in the export department, and Mum in the local old folks' home, so everyone knew. Of course Dad got out of it quick, but Mum got sympathy and dirty looks in about equal proportions.

I was the "innocent victim," and it got right up my nose. Overnight people stopped seeing me as David Winterbourne, responsible for my own actions, person in his own right, et cetera et cetera. Everything I did was different because of Mum and Dad. First of all, because I went on as usual, I was taking it well. I was a little angel. That made me think there was something funny about living just with Mum and seeing Dad every Saturday, so I tried throwing a few tantrums to bring them back together again. Instead of a cuff round the ear from Dad, all I got was sorrowful looks, understanding chats, an extra bag of malted milk balls. I was only twelve then, so you can't blame me for seeing I was onto a good thing.

Dad caught on pretty soon, mind. He was at El Alamein in the war—I narrowly missed getting myself christened with the name Montgomery—and he was a great one for self-discipline. He said somebody had to teach it to you first, though, which generally meant doing without supper or going without candy money. That was when he was still at home, of course. After the sorrowful-looks period, he took to kind of flicking me on the top of my jawbone just under the earlobe. It hurt enough to remind me to behave, but not enough to make me feel a fool.

Anyway, there was Miss Ruskin sitting across the tile-topped table, looking at me with her human brown eyes and waiting. And if she was hoping to get a true human confession out of me about the difficulties of living in a broken home, she had another think coming.

I said in my two-tone voice, "I didn't know it was against the rules to go to the can."

Her eye muscles crinkled again. She said without expression, "You were smoking, David."

"Yes."

I'd learned that from Dad. Just a flat monosyllable, no excuses or apologies. That's how he was when he finally said he was leaving. Maybe Miss Ruskin would get like poor old Mum now and start flapping and protesting. But she didn't.

"D'you often smoke?"

"No."

"How often?"

Her brown eyes looked straight at me. I couldn't hold the stare, so I let my gaze flick at the window. It was dripping with rain.

"Twenty a week."

It was a lie. Dad caught me with a butt when I was seven and stood over me while I smoked a king size. I've never bothered about smoking since. I wasn't even inhaling in the lavatory. Jasper gave me this hand-rolled one, and it was something to do while I waited for the rain to

4

put an end to the Games period.

"That makes quite a hole in your paper-round money, doesn't it?"

She was taking it well, I'll give her that. Mind you, she was paid not to be shocked. I considered telling her I nicked them from Woolworth's but decided that might have repercussions, so I just shrugged.

"It's a mug's game, David, you must know that. You're underage but I suppose no one can stop you smoking if you really want to. Except you yourself." Now that *did* sound like Dad. The self-discipline stuff again. "So ask yourself if you really want to go on with it. Keep asking. Never mind who else smokes. Just ask yourself every time you have a cigarette whether you really want to get hooked on a pointless habit that might end up in a terrible illness."

I looked back at her, down at her fingers. No, she didn't smoke. That was something. The number of grown-ups who gave you that sort of chat and lit up immediately you walked out of the room—it made me sick, that did.

She seemed to relax a bit.

"Well, that's it, David. I suppose I ought to tell you off, but what's the point? You know the score as well as I do. You broke a school rule. That means a loss of privilege, probably a detention. Mr. Eccles will sort that out with you." Eccles was head of the P.E. department. "Rules are for your own protection, so you may well have hurt yourself in some way. But when it comes to the crunch we can't stop you breaking rules and damaging yourself. It's up to you." She sat back in her chair and tightened her mouth in a funny half grin. "So there we are. . . . Now, I've been meaning to see you since half term about your environmental study."

In the fourth year we were supposed to have another shot at Environmental Studies "in depth," as they put it. In other words, we'd had a look at where we lived during the first year—a sort of do-it-yourself local geography course. Now we chose some particular aspect of our town and spent one day a week examining it thoroughly so we could come up with a report at the end of term. Miss Ruskin was supposed to get us chatting about our interests and then "channel" them in a certain direction and ring up people we could interview or observe or something. It was just a waste of time like everything else. Some of the goodies enjoyed it, of course. There was nursing for the girls—Mum had to put up with some of them at the Home. There was preschool play-group stuff. Voluntary welfare work of all kinds. It was up to you to come up with whatever you fancied. Jasper had told me he was going to investigate single-parent families and I'd hit him. That was how he came to give me the cig, to make up for it.

I looked at Miss Ruskin. It was nice of her to change the subject to something safe and uninteresting. I made a noise in my throat, which was meant to indicate I hadn't got the remotest idea of what to do for my study.

She let her grin grow a bit.

"It's okay; no one ever knows what to do at first. Any ideas for your future career?"

"I thought about the Army."

"Did you now? Well, there's one possibility. I could arrange a talk with the recruiting officer. And there might

6

be a chance of going along to observe some training." She shuffled with some papers in a briefcase by her feet and came up with a form. I thought I saw "Winterbourne" on the top of it. "I see your mother works with geriatrics."

There it was again, the personal approach. And I didn't like the term "geriatrics" much, either. Why should old people be called geriatrics? Any more than single-parent families be called innocent victims? I grunted again.

"How about looking into their problems?"

"No, thanks."

It wasn't the old people. I've been with Mum to the Home and some of them were great. Terrific characters. But I couldn't stand seeing Mum working with them and knowing she'd got to go on doing it till she drew the pension. When I left school, Dad and me between us could have given Mum a break, but not me on my own.

"Your mother would be most helpful. Able to give the other point of view—"

"No, thanks," I repeated belligerently.

She got the message. "Okay. I'll talk to the Army recruiting place then, and see if there's anyone else who'd like to come along with you. Keep your eyes and ears open, David. There's a lot going on in the world these days." She fumbled around in her case again, putting away the form, which probably now said I was going into the Army. So next open night it would be mentioned to Mum, who would have kittens because I've never breathed a word about it at home. But I'll have to get away. Okay, so it's like Dad, scramming off and leaving Mum. But I'll have to go.

Anyway, Miss Ruskin stood up and we wandered out

into the corridor and bumped straight into Eccles, sopping wet in his rugby gear with a towel draped over his head. He barked at me, and Miss Ruskin said hastily she'd better go but we'd talked and sorted out quite a few things. Eccles softened slightly, handed me out a double detention and a few threats about the dire consequences of missing a good game in the pouring rain and cleared off. I chased after Miss Ruskin's brown skirt and sweater and long hair and caught sight of it all going into the Sixth Form block. They were putting on *The Mikado*, and she was one of the three little maids from school. They had all the luck in the sixth and seventh years. If you could hang on that long.

I wandered on down to the showers. It was nearly the end of the afternoon, so I hadn't done too badly even with the double detention. The noise in the shower room was deafening and someone was running around with Jasper's clothes while he howled loudly from behind the canvas curtain. I backed out and went on into the Common room.

A few of the girls were there already because they'd cut hockey—they could get away with anything. Mart Coles, who had a hole in his heart or something, was sitting by the window playing Scrabble with Jess Henshawe. Mart was terrific at chess and Scrabble and cribbage—games like that—and Jess was supposed to play Scrabble because her spelling was all up the creek, but I bet she was having a hard time of it that day. She was a smashing gymnast with the sort of figure you'd expect in a leotard, and a face like a slice of Madeira cake—good but plain. No reason for her shyness, really; she blushed if you looked at her.

8

I went over and looked at the board. Mart had a lousy hand. He made RAT into RATE and scored himself four. Jess fingered an s and two E's off her rack and eyed the open T.

"D'you spell 'seat' with two E's?" she asked Mart.

He gave one of his snorty laughs and I picked up her letters which she dropped in confusion, and stuck them on the end of RATE to make RATES and SEE. That gave her two words and a double score. She couldn't thank me, though. She went puce and concentrated on writing down her score while Mart snarled at me to clear off and find my own game.

It was time to go anyway. The others were trickling in with hair still wet, sneezing and yelling at me because I'd got out of it and they hadn't. If I did my paper round before tea, I could go out tonight and let Mum think I was doing it then. I never did anything when I went out at night. Just hung around the chip shop and talked to Jasper and looked at the bingo queues and wondered what it was all about.

That was what Miss Ruskin had said—"What's it all about?" If she didn't know, how did she expect me to tell her?

2

That's the school bit. It was like that most days, with decent interludes in the metal and woodwork rooms or the swimming pool. And boring sessions called discussion groups. I rarely discovered what we were discussing. Mart Coles and his lot did most of the talking; Jasper usually played cards at the back and sometime or other some bright boy would decide to enliven things with a fart, so the place smelled pretty bad. We had to stay on at school till we were sixteen and they didn't know what to do with us, and a lot of us felt it wasn't our job to help them out.

The home bit's more difficult to describe because of this feeling of *sorrow* I had for Mum. I nearly wrote down pity, but it was more than that. She'd done the wrong thing marrying Dad and having me. I wanted to help her out somehow but I didn't know how, and in any case I felt guilty about it all. So often I got angry with her, especially if she looked tired or sad, and then I'd go out in case I went and said something to hurt her more.

That was how it was that night. I finished the papers and got in just before she did. In time to make a pot of tea and get the cloth on the table—Mum's funny like that, she doesn't mind if nothing's on the cloth so long as it's over the table.

She sat with her elbows on the table and her hair damp and flat from wearing a head scarf. She sipped her tea as if it were rare whisky or nectar or something and said, as per usual, "What should we do without a cup of tea?"

I laughed, also as usual, and ferreted in her bag to see what we were going to eat. There was a packet of fish fingers and some crinkle-cut chips and a plastic bag oozing with gooey liver.

"That's for tomorrow," Mum said. "I'll put it in the

oven tonight. We'll have the fish and chips in a minute. Soon as I've finished my tea and recovered. Of course I went without my umbrella this morning."

"Me, too," I said, hoping she'd grin. And she did. So I followed it up by dropping the liver bag on the floor and pretending it was my guts. But that was going too far.

"You wouldn't think that was funny if you saw some of the things I saw," she said. She told me about some poor old bloke without legs who had fallen out of bed that morning and started his one stump off bleeding. I felt terrible.

"Done your homework?" she followed up.

"Yep." I could catch up on it tomorrow night during my double detention.

"So you've got to go out after tea and do your paper round," she grumbled, hoisting herself up to go to the kitchen.

"Yep," I said again.

Mum glanced at my damp trouser legs and then away. She must have known I was lying, but she wasn't going to say anything. Sometimes I could understand why Dad left us.

Jasper and Rorie McClune were alone under the street-lamp outside the chip shop. It was still raining and the gutters gleamed and rippled with reflections.

"Got any money, Wint?" Jasper greeted me, again as per usual. "We could go down the cafe and play pinball."

"Fivepence." I'd hoped to buy a batter-dipped sausage with that. Mum's fish fingers and crinkle cuts hadn't filled me.

11

"We could go to the Youth Club and play pinball," Rorie objected. "They won't chuck us out there for not buying any food."

Jasper didn't take kindly to that. People like Mart Coles and Jess Henshawe went to the Youth Club.

We stood haggling and getting wet. Two girls went past and Jasper broke off to whistle them. When they ignored us, he blew a raspberry. They were a couple of girls from the convent, far above us, secure in their special world.

Jasper told us a joke and we roared laughing, though it wasn't a bit funny. We wanted those girls to think we were secure and special, too. We wanted them to envy us. Because really we were envying them. It came to me suddenly. Jasper and Rorie didn't know it. But we were all three standing there in the rain with nothing to do, envying those girls who were off to choir practice or vespers or whatever convent girls go to.

Jasper told another joke and this time we didn't laugh, because the girls couldn't hear us anymore, so he got nasty and told us he was fed up with the pair of us. That was the place where normally we'd either drift off together to the Youth Club or the cafe, or I'd clear off on my own and look at the bingo queues or work out whether the installment plan terms on the color tellies in the electric shop were more economic than the hiring charges. Don't laugh, I've been considering getting one when I leave school. Well, all Mum does besides work is watch telly.

Anyway, that wasn't what happened that night. Not quite. Old Buff Harkins rolled up out of the rain in his cycling cape and sou'wester, looking like that ad for sardines. Buff's got no special friends, but with his daft ways and amiable grin he's on good terms with everyone and moves from the Mart Coles set down to Jasper's lot without offending anyone on the way. His parents throw pots or something weird in a farm laborer's cottage on the moors, and Buff comes to school in batik-dyed shirts and homemade trousers.

Jasper's irritability vanished at the sight of him.

"Hi, Buff. What y'doing in the bright lights then?"

Buff grinned at the sarcasm and looked up at us from under the brim of his huge hat.

"Rita and Joe are having a quick one while I get fish and chips all round. Celebration."

Rita and Joe were Mr. and Mrs. Harkins.

"Won the pools?" Rorie inquired eagerly.

"Oh, sure. Twice over. No, Jem's sold his first picture."

We were unimpressed. Jem Harkins must be twenty now; we could barely remember him in the fifth year when we were in the first. A couple of years ago, he had quietly dropped out of art college and gone to live in some derelict cottage in North Devon to paint.

Buff sensed our apathy.

"He's had enough of roughing it on his own, at least through the winter. He suggested I took a couple of days off school and hitched down there with some of my mates." He looked at me. "How about it, Winnie?"

Jasper said, "Hey. We'd be like hippies, man!"

Rorie blew a raspberry. "Hippies only exist in the summer. This is—like—November, man."

We all curled up laughing. Buff spluttered through the drips on his hat, "Maybe that's where they go in the wintertime. Like flies. There's quite a colony down there. Jem says a couple of groups rent an old farmhouse where they can practice undisturbed."

Jasper looked really interested. "Sounds quite a scene. You serious, Buff? What about it, Wint?"

I looked at Buff wondering what Rita and Joe, not to mention Jem, would think of the four of us hitching to North Devon. But Buff was really hooked on the idea; his small dark eyes flashed enthusiasm under that flipping hat.

Jasper spoke into my hesitation. "Can't leave Mummy on her own. . . ." His voice was high and lisping. "She wouldn't like me asking strange men for lifts—"

I caught him in the solar plexus. Not hard, but he doubled up dramatically and pretended to throw up in the gutter.

Buff laughed. He should have been a diplomat—maybe he would be one day.

"Got to go, kids. But think it over. Give it thought. Due consideration. Pontificate. Like crazy. Okay?"

He went into the chip shop and we watched him tuck an enormous newspaper parcel under the cape and then buy a fivepence bag, which he handed to us. He was a good kid. Then Rita and Joe rolled up in the old jalopy they'd bought for Buff's thirteenth birthday—some present—and took him off.

Jasper went on fermenting with hip talk for about ten minutes. According to him, we'd go to North Devon next week with sleeping bags and guitars and before we knew it we'd be discovered and appear on telly, and the only thing between us and the girl fans would be our sacks of money. Loot. Like . . . bread, man.

14

It wouldn't come to anything. Rorie and I knew that—probably Jasper knew it, too. Buff might get away with taking someone like Mart Coles and it would become an educational thing, an exercise in self-sufficiency, et cetera et cetera, blah-blah-blah. But not with Jasper or Rorie or me.

But we had a laugh talking about it. And eating Buff's chips. Then I told them how I'd wrapped Miss Ruskin round my little finger that afternoon and I had more than a suspicion that she fancied me. And I added that Jasper could keep his hand-rolled cigs in future and stuff 'em up his sweater. Only I didn't say sweater.

And then I went home and got out of my wet gear and watched the ten-o'clock news with Mum.

That was the home bit.

3

Friday and the double detention came and went, and I expected Saturday to be as usual, with Dad picking me up about eleven-thirty in time for lunch, then football or the pictures or a drive somewhere. But it wasn't quite like that.

I vaguely heard Mum leave at ten to eight; then the next thing I knew Dad's dot-dot-dot, dash-dash-dash, dot-dot-dot ring was going on the doorbell. Save Our Souls. He's a great one for the epigrams is Dad, and if he can't say them he knocks them out in Morse.

He wasn't very pleased to see me still in my pajamas.

"Wouldn't hurt you on a Saturday morning to get up with your mother and spend a couple of hours cleaning the place through."

I used to think his concern for Mum was a good sign; part of me deep down still did.

"She doesn't like the way I do it—says she can never find a thing after I've tidied up. I go to the launderette. Make my bed. Things like that."

He didn't look delighted but he said, "Fair enough. Get yourself washed and dressed then. I'll make some coffee and toast."

"Crisp and not much butter for me." I grinned at him as he aimed a swipe at my head. It was great to see old Dad. We had this easy, surface relationship. I went on, very laconic, "What's on the program?"

"Something special." He lit the grill and unhooked a couple of mugs from the cupboard. I noticed he was wearing his best suit. Also that it made him look quite with-it. Much younger than Mum. "Snack lunch 'cause we're visiting for tea and we'll have to do justice to it."

That meant Gran's. Dad's mother. She didn't like it if you left one dab of sauce on your plate. Not that I ever did.

I swung upstairs and thought that that meant the suit was for a concert or something else to improve the mind that afternoon. Not that I minded. It was so easy being with Dad. The main thing was, I didn't have to feel sorry for him or responsible for him or anything. But also he just told me what to do and I did it. Whether he was teaching me self-discipline or what, I don't know. But it was restful.

16

Mind you, after he told me what was happening I had a choice. For instance, when we were driving into Bristol he said, "Where d'you want to go for our snack?"

And I said, "Somewhere up Park Street. Let's have a pasta like we did when Uncle Phil was with us."

And he said, "Okay."

If I'd said fish and chips in the car or a packet of sandwiches down at the docks, he'd still have said okay. But it was no good trying to alter the afternoon arrangements. He nearly always fixed those by buying tickets, or if not, he'd say we were going somewhere to have a chat. If ever I said I wanted to see a particular film, he'd find out about it in the week and we'd go the following Saturday. Or we wouldn't go if he didn't like the sound of it.

Anyway, I knew better than to quibble when he handed over two tickets to an exhibition of dance at the Albert Rooms starting at two o'clock that afternoon.

I did pull a face, though, as I pushed them back into his half of the glove compartment.

"What's up?" he said, pulling one back.

I had to laugh. "Kid stuff," I said. "We do it at school. It's called dance-drama. Last week I had to be an onion and unpeel."

"Bet you made everyone cry." He glanced in the mirror, flipped the indicator and passed an E-type Jaguar. I chortled approval. "Did you read the ticket properly? The kids who are putting on the display are paraplegic."

I reached for the tickets again. It just said the children from Underwood School were presenting a display of dance on Saturday the fifteenth of November at two o'clock and contributions would go to the school funds.

"What's para . . . whatever you said?"

"Paralyzed from the waist down. But Underwood has spastics, too."

It clicked now. Underwood was a special school. I'd always thought it was for nut cases.

I said glumly, "Sounds great."

Dad said, "It might be embarrassing. I've no idea. I've been told to go in with a completely open mind."

"What made you choose it? You haven't been talking to Miss Ruskin?" I suddenly had a nasty mental picture of her on the phone saying how little interest David took in his school life and how very difficult it was for him coping with separated parents. If she did anything like that, she'd have had it as far as I was concerned. Brown eyes, straight dark hair—the lot.

Dad said, "Who the hell's Miss Ruskin?"

I relaxed. "No one. Just a teacher. What made you choose it?"

"Someone I know works there. The tickets are complimentary."

"Oh." I looked again. No price, just the bit about contributions, so they'd probably pass the hat round. "Oh, yes."

It must cost Dad a bomb taking me out every Saturday and I generally knew when he was hard up, because those were the days we just had a drive and a chat. What between the snack lunch, free afternoon and tea at Gran's, he must be pretty well broke.

We parked the car in a multistory garage, which was great because it always made me think of an Alfred Hitchcock film. Then we walked past the University, looked at the secondhand books in those little shops at the top of Park Street and strolled on down to the first Italian place we came to.

It wasn't raining, but a ceiling of gray cloud sat on top of the roofs and the air was damp and cold on our faces. It made you realize Christmas wasn't far away and I couldn't help a wriggle of excitement in my chest, although Christmas is even duller than most days since Dad left.

We ate our pasta, and Dad kept calling the waiter "Luigi" just when I was drinking my water so I nearly sprayed a mouthful all over the place. The waiter played along and put *a*'s on the end of all his words.

"You like-a the whipped-a cream and fruit, signor?" he asked after I'd mopped up the last of my sauce with a wedge of bread roll.

Dad goes, "Twice over, please, Luigi," so he couldn't be that short. We heard Luigi shout through the door in a Birmingham accent, "Two fruits and milk and make it snappy, Sid." I was trying to get a drink again and I nearly choked.

After the dessert, we sat a bit over our coffee and Dad asked the usual questions about was I all right, was Mum all right, was there anything needed doing to the house. I answered yes to the first two, no to the third. Then I waffled on about school—Dad likes to hear about that—but I didn't mention Miss Ruskin or Buff Harkins's idea about going to North Devon. The one was over and the other wouldn't happen anyway. But I'd have liked to tell him. I couldn't tell Mum, because she'd start flapping and going into it all. But Dad would have grinned and told me to keep my nose clean. Trouble was, if I didn't tell

Mum, it wouldn't be fair to tell Dad, would it?

Then I asked about Uncle Phil—Dad's brother—and Gran and Gramps and Dad's job. We had our usual chat, except that I knew Dad wanted to say something and wasn't sure how to come out with it. It's often like that. When it's Mum's birthday and he wants to give me some money to buy her something decent, he goes all round the mulberry bush to get to it.

At last he said, "Time we were going, Dave." He got up and we went to the cash desk to pay. Then he said, "Margaret Daly—the woman I was telling you about who works at Underwood—she wants us to go to tea at her place after."

It hit me like a series of elbow jabs in a scrum. Not all at once. One after the other, but all in the same place so it hurt worse and worse. First of all, fairly superficial . . . We had to go to tea with a stranger, which meant no real hard eating on my part. Then the stranger was a woman, moreover a woman Dad could call Margaret. And we were going to this dancing exhibition thing because she worked with the kids.

I wanted to ask a lot of questions. There was more to this. But I had the feeling the answers would be more elbow jabs, and in any case, what exactly could I ask? "Who is she? How did you meet her? What is your relationship . . . ?"

As I trailed out of the cafe after Dad, I told myself there was nothing to it. So what if Dad had got to know a rotten old teacher at a special school and was doing her a favor by going to her rotten display? He probably thought the teatime discussion would be good for me— how the other half lives or something.

But I didn't like it. I didn't like it one bit.

The old 'Bert Rooms were almost full when we went in. They'd been built for assemblies when Bristol was a spa, and there were two galleries running round the walls already lined with people. Chairs were arranged around the perimeter of the floor, with a big clear space in the middle. We found a couple of empty ones and sat down. Dad looked nervous. He leaned forward with his elbows on his knees and rubbed his chin. I joined him.

"How can they dance when they're paralyzed from the waist down?" I murmured out of the side of my mouth.

"Dunno. But remember what I said about an open mind."

I wondered whether he meant something more than just this performance. My pasta seemed to be disagreeing with the fruit salad and I felt sick.

A woman came on and said something inaudible. I knew from Dad's sudden tension that this was Margaret Daly. A man hurried toward her carrying a mike on a stand and trailing a snake of cable. There was a ripple of laughter. She took the mike and it crackled and spat, and she made a small helpless gesture with her one hand held out to us palm upward. Dad's face suddenly softened.

"Ladies and gentlemen—" There were children in the audience and she laughed breathlessly: *Families* . . . I apologize for this bad beginning. We've rehearsed, but not actually in this hall, so you must forgive . . ." She went on for a bit. The aims of the school, the creative ideas that could be stimulated by this form of movement. Et cetera. The first piece was called "The Forest"

21

and the children had made most of the props by themselves. With help. Blah-blah.

She turned and made a signal, and through the open door to the foyer a string of wheelchairs whirled into the old ballroom manned by kids of about twelve, all holding between their teeth great long chiffon scarf things. They whizzed all over the place, in and out, never coming anywhere near a crash but just going where they wanted. And the scarves streamed out behind them, sometimes weaving one with another, sometimes flapping up and down, then trailing on the floor, until the room seemed full of whirling green chiffon. And the kids made a sound, too. Sort of hissing through their teeth. And with the rush of their rubber-tired wheels on the floor, it sounded like a high wind.

Then they stopped hissing and slowed down until they stopped. Then they covered their heads with the scarves and let the ends trail down over their fingers. They were grinning like mad and looking all round at us, but at last they got themselves covered up and still. At some time or other, everyone who does dance-drama has to be a tree and I've seen worse ones. Much worse ones.

Next thing that happened was a loud clumping sound like a chair being banged up and down on the floor. Through the door appeared a huge cardboard cutout of an elephant, its legs not quite concealing the chrome driving wheels of another pair of wheelchairs. The elephant moved stolidly over to a tree and stopped. Then there was a roar and in came a lion. Then some coconuts were clip-clopped and a horse with a braided-wool tail galloped shakily into the shade of a palm. Then a West Indian girl, with her hair in about a hundred braids, slid in on her tummy, commando fashion, trailing a lumpy tube of material. In case we didn't get the message, she stopped halfway across the arena and hissed through her grinning teeth. She curled her long appendage around another tree and propped her head on an elbow to study our reactions.

That was it. Somewhere a tambourine rattled and the animals made their exit, to tumultuous applause, closely followed by the wind-shaken trees.

Dad looked at me. His face was wide open. "My God," he said. "My God, Dave. Makes you think, eh?"

I remembered to clap; then I glanced around covertly so I wouldn't have to look at Dad's face. Everyone was smiling; some of the women had a job to hold on to theirs. Those kids were something.

Then the woman came back.

Dad whispered, "She works three mornings a week with them. That's all. Just three mornings." I stopped clapping.

People were quiet and she started to say something but I didn't listen. I looked at her; really looked. Trying to see what Dad saw in her. She was taller than Mum, one of those very skinny women whose cheek and jawbones show prominent in their faces. She had on a round-necked sweater and trousers, both gray wool, and above the sweater her Adam's apple was plainly visible, and at the end of each sleeve her wrists were long and bony. Her hair was mouse brown and lay quietly on either side of her forehead like the picture of Charlotte Brontë in the frontispiece of the school biography.

If that sounds unattractive, then I've done well. She was unattractive. Not a bit like Mum, who is round and

23

sweet like an apple and homely and nice. I was shaken. Right to my foundations. I didn't feel like that when Dad left, I suppose because I never really thought it was permanent, but I didn't. I'd never felt like this before. I hated Margaret Daly.

Anyway the display thing went on. The first lot of kids came in without their chairs, pulling themselves along on the floor like seals. Then they did a lot of swimming and rolling movements. They were good, but it was their faces that really made it go. I've never seen kids look so darned happy and proud about anything. If only it hadn't been for Margaret Daly, I'd have really enjoyed myself.

Then Dad tensed up again.

"The finale," he said to me under cover of the applause. "These are Maggie's speciality. The spastic children."

I sat back away from him and clenched my hands inside my parka. How I hated her. Maggie.

The wheelchairs came on, just four of them. These were pushed by four adults. Each kid held a bunch of balloons—I found out after that the balloons were tied to their wrists, because their grip, like all their muscular movement, was spasmodic. The balloons were filled with hydrogen, not all at the same pressure, and the kids and their adult drivers were almost lost in a welter of pastel spheres. The chairs went round and round in a figure eight and the balloons leapt and danced from the frantic, windmill arms of those kids. They couldn't control them, they didn't try. For once, their crazy jerky gesticulations made sense. They shouted and shrieked with the joy of it, and their hoarse inarticulate voices made the audience laugh and clap for them almost incessantly.

24

I was terrified Dad was going to cry. He had hold of the chair in front of him and he was staring at those kids with all his eyes. Almost as if he was willing them to go on whirling the balloons and enjoying themselves so much.

Then they were gone, and cups of tea were being passed down the rows and daft little sandwiches about the size of a stamp. Dad jerked his head at me and stood up, and we excused ourselves past four pairs of nylon knees.

She appeared from nowhere.

"Well?" She had brown eyes like tea without milk, and Dad must have been able to see right to the bottom of them the way she looked up at him.

He took her hand—it was stretched toward him with the palm up as it had been stretched toward us all before, sort of supplicating—and probably squeezed it, because she immediately relaxed and smiled socially.

"This is my son, Maggie." He sort of pulled the hand in my direction, and I found I was holding it. It was very hot and damp. "David, this is Mrs. Daly, who is responsible for what we have just seen."

"That's not strictly true, David." I tried to look away from her smile and could not. "I simply assembled the available talent."

I made one of my throat noises and tried to unglue my hand.

Dad said, "It was great, Maggie. Simply great. Wasn't it, Dave?"

"Yes." I got my hand free and rubbed it surreptitiously on my backside.

She said in what was supposed to be a simple, sincere

voice, "I'm glad. Thank you very much, both of you."

Someone else came up, and in about two seconds we were all surrounded by people congratulating Mrs. Daly on her wonderful work. The foyer doors were opened again and wheelchairs came back in and were claimed by proud parents. Everyone was milling around. Dad stood there grinning like an idiot and sort of laying claim to Daly as if he was her manager or something.

I knew I couldn't stand it. Not for another two or even three hours. More little sandwiches in a fancy flat somewhere and Dad breathing adoration all over the place. I should puke up or something.

So I left. It was easy; no one even saw me go. I even put a fivepence bit in a fruit dish stuck on a card table in the foyer. Then I ran for the bus center and got on the first bus back home.

The November afternoon pressed against the bus windows and in the teatime twilight the shopwindows winked a welcome. But I didn't feel Christmassy anymore. Just lonely.

4

Of course as I let myself in the front door the phone was going like crazy and it was Dad.

"What's going on?" he snapped. It was nearly five-thirty; he'd probably been looking for me over an hour.

I made my voice even throatier than usual.

"That pasta . . . I thought I was going to throw up."

There was a pause while he tried to sum me up. He decided to believe me.

"You could have let me know what you were doing." He didn't sound too aggrieved. Of course he'd had Maggie to console him. "We looked everywhere. Mrs. Daly is very disappointed. She was looking forward to getting to know you."

It was all such a put-up job. I could imagine them planning it together. She would know with those clear tea-brown eyes of hers that the kids in their wheelchairs would soften me up. It would be something to talk about, to break the ice. Over the crab paste and cucumber, she would tell Dad and me about her work, and we would all become jolly good friends. I could just see my dim reflection in the dark hall mirror and I gave it a vicious V sign.

"Sorry about it, Dad. Look, I've got to lie down."

"Isn't your mother in?"

"Not yet. Any minute. D'you want to talk to her?"

"No. I don't like you being alone. Will you be all right?"

"Course. Cheerio, Dad. Thanks for lunch." I wasn't going to thank him for anything else. Anything else at all.

"All right, son." He sounded very tired all of a sudden. "I'll pick you up same time next week."

The worst bit was when Mum came in and I told her. She looked very perky in her orange head scarf tucked in the high collar of her tweed coat. She was dead pleased to see me.

"David. You're early. Isn't that nice—we'll have some beans on toast and watch *The Generation Game.* Is the kettle on?"

"No." I wanted to make her as miserable as I was. She had no right to come bouncing in like one of those hydrogen-filled balloons, making the best of her rotten life. Beans on toast and telly. That was her idea of a great evening.

I blurted it straight out while she stood there unbuttoning her coat.

"I came home early. Dad's got a woman up there. He's all over her."

She went very still for a minute. She sort of looked through me. Her eyes were blank. Then she sucked in some air and shrugged off her coat. She focused again and smiled slightly.

"It's only natural, Dave. He's not forty yet." She put her coat on a hanger and hooked it on the picture rail where it would air off. With her back to me, she said, "Is she free? Free to marry him, I mean?"

I hadn't thought of that. "Her name is *Mrs.* Daly." I thought back over what Dad had said. "No husband was mentioned. I don't know."

"I wonder." She bent down and switched on the second bar of the electric fire. She looked frozen; sort of pinched up. "Dad ought to marry again. He must be so lonely."

I felt like I'd just missed an easy pass on the football field. *Dad* lonely?

28

"He's got Gran and Gramps," I said.

"They haven't stopped being angry with him for leaving. He's got no one of his own."

"Poor old Dad," I said, heavily sarcastic.

She flushed slightly. "It's impossible for you to understand, Dave. It was no one's fault—us splitting up—just one of those things."

We'd had this conversation before. Endlessly.

"Look, Mum—" I began desperately.

Then she said with devastating honesty, "I know how you feel, David. I feel the same. It's just jealousy. . . . You hate her, don't you?"

I stared and then nodded dumbly. I wasn't sure I liked Mum talking like this. Some things were better left in the dark.

"So do I. But it's daft, love. Dad deserves another chance at a happy marriage. He really does. He'd make a good husband with the right woman." She sighed and turned toward the kitchen to open the baked beans. I thought that was it. But it wasn't. She paused at the door and stared down the hall as if she was saying good-bye to someone.

"Funny thing, Dave. I suppose I've always thought one day we'd have another try. Ah, well." She laughed, and added sort of apologetically, "You've got an idiot mother."

I spent most of Sunday feeling like a murderer or something. I took Mum a cup of tea in bed and didn't have Radio One all morning, and at dinnertime I made sure not to shovel my food. But I still felt lousy.

Then on Monday morning when Jasper was nagging Buffy Harkins about the North Devon trip—Buffy was already soft-peddling, so I guessed his parents were fixing it up legal-like—he used a phrase that stuck in my mind.

"Look here, Buff," he said, all adult. "You've got to stop thinking up the snags. Think positive, man. We're going. Okay? Let's start from there."

Think positive.

I seemed to see the words written in neon. Think positive.

Mum hated Maggie Daly and so did I. But we weren't doing a damned thing about it. We didn't even know if there was a husband in the background or anything. We had to think positive. And act.

Until break, I was in the lab making up slides for the third year. That was another thing we did to fill in time—act as unpaid lab technicians. But it gave me time to think. Positive.

What did I know about Mrs. Margaret Daly? What she looked like and where she worked. That was all.

At break, I made for the staff room and hung around till Miss Ruskin hove in sight. She was wearing jeans and a paint-smeared smock.

"Could I have a word?" It sounded brusque, almost insulting. Everything I said sounded like that somehow.

"Certainly." She tried to push back her hair with hands that smelled of turpentine. "I ought to clean up first, though. What are you doing after break?"

"Art." Which probably meant cleaning about a million hard brushes for the Lower School.

30

"Good." She nodded briskly. "You can come and help me paint the *Mikado* flats and we can talk. Will that do?"

I grinned, really pleased. It's easier to talk when you're working together and I was dying to tell someone about those kids on Saturday afternoon. I couldn't very well tell Mum, could I? And the only person who'd be interested at school was Buff Harkins, and he was avoiding me at the moment because of the Devon business.

At first it was hopeless. She got me an old shirt and we went over to the Sixth Form block together; then about half a dozen superior types joined us and kept calling her Jackie and quoting bits from the script, so I felt like they meant me to. An outsider.

She seemed to play along with them a bit, and then she said, "Look. Marilyn. Jock. Can you cope with that willow on your own? Remember, all blue and white. David and I will just sit here and do a few coolie hats while we chat."

That got rid of them without any hard feelings, and we squatted on the floor with a pile of flat cardboard shapes, which we stapled into hats and then painted with black enamel and pegged on a line to dry. It was restful.

She told me some of the story of *The Mikado* and how nearly all Gilbert and Sullivan operas were spoofs. So those old boys weren't so square.

Then she said, "I've been in touch with the recruiting people in Bristol and there's a lot of things you can go and see, David. They'll give you a list when you call on them—with dates—and if you jot them down it'll be quite easy to arrange time off for you."

31

I felt myself go hot.

"Thanks, Miss. But I—I sort of changed my mind."

She looked up in surprise. Of course, next to that Sixth Form lot I sounded the biggest yobbo in the world.

"I mean—I'm still interested in the Army and I'll probably join when I leave school. But for this study thing, I thought . . ."

"You're welcome to change your mind, David." She gave me that nice half smile that wasn't all intimate. It suddenly struck me why I liked her. She never told me any details of her life—her personal life, I mean. She kept her privacy and she let me keep mine. There was this teacher a couple of years ago who kept telling me how his wife misunderstood him. Probably waiting for me to confide details of Mum and Dad's rows.

"What did you have in mind?"

I concentrated on painting a hat and started to tell her about the Underwood kids. When I got to the bit about the balloons, I was damned near crying.

She said musingly, "How lucky we are. I wonder whether we owe them something?"

I said, "Not specially. Not just because they're para . . . paraplegic."

"You don't like special names for people, do you, David? I noticed how you curled up when I referred to your mother's patients as geriatrics."

"Well . . ." I got up and pegged my hat on the line, took another and stapled it. "It's all right if you still treat them as ordinary people. But if you help them just because they're old or can't walk, then . . . I don't know. It's not right." People were often nice to me because I was an innocent victim. But I knew they didn't like me really. And I hated that.

She said, "They're being kind for the wrong reasons then. Is that what you mean? To make *themselves* feel good."

I nodded. That must be it. That's what made them two-faced even when they were doing you a good turn.

She said, "Why do you want to visit Underwood, David?"

I couldn't very well tell her I wanted to find out something about one of the teachers, but I didn't want to lie either.

I said, "I want to find out about the kind of people who help them. Teachers and so on."

"Yes. That's quite a thought. Whether they're helping for altruistic reasons. Or for some kind of self-glory."

I didn't know what altruistic meant but I nodded anyway. She went on a bit about compassion and a kind of objective love called "agape," and I kept nodding and painting.

Then she said, "Funny this should have happened, David. I've already telephoned Underwood and arranged for someone from your class to visit them. This afternoon, as a matter of fact. Did you know that?"

She looked at me directly, obviously wondering if I was trying to pull a fast one. But my surprise must have looked genuine. Actually I was horrified. I wanted to do this job strictly on my own.

She seemed satisfied. "No reason why you shouldn't go along together. You'll probably find it helpful to have someone to talk it over with. Try to relate to one child

33

and one adult if you can. And start with the child. Get talking—anything will do—their work or hobbies—"

I listened and went on nodding. At last I managed to get a word in.

"Who is it going with me, Miss?" If it was anyone except Buff Harkins, I couldn't face it.

"Jess Henshawe," said Miss Ruskin without any expression at all. "She's considering a living-in job there for next summer." She went over to the drying hats and touched them experimentally. "These first few are dry, David. Could you stack them to make room for the others? I must go and see how Marilyn and Jock are getting on with their willow."

Which, I suppose, was as good a way as any of saying she didn't want to chat anymore.

5

Jess and me caught the one-thirty bus to Bristol and sat in the sideways seat behind the driver like a couple of stuffed dummies. I knew Jess wouldn't speak unless I did, and I had more important things to think about than making conversation. Of course in our school uniforms we were marked out like escaped prisoners, and it was a laugh to hear the comments from some of the passengers as they paid the driver. Some eyed us as if we were unexploded bombs and said belligerently, "What are those

34

two doing here during school hours?" Others smiled sentimentally and said in stage whispers, "Aren't they sweet—sitting there so quiet and good." If Jess had been a different sort, we could have had a giggle. But she wasn't and we didn't.

I was beginning to wonder what the hell I was doing here anyway. I remembered Daly only worked at Underwood for three mornings, so at least I shouldn't run into her, but if Miss Ruskin arranged a morning appointment next time I'd be right up the creek. And how on earth did I think I could casually bring up her name? "Oh, excuse me, have you got a Mrs. Daly here? No, I don't know her and please don't mention my name to her in case she thinks I do. . . ."

Jess was tugging my sleeve like a little kid.

"Would it be better to get off here?" she whispered, red faced. "We could cut up Church Road to the Heights—" She noticed me noticing a big spot on the side of her nose and went puce.

I dragged my eyes away from her face. "Okay." I stood up and the driver grinned sideways at me.

"Going up the woods, eh? Good hunting."

I thought Jess would drop dead. Somehow we both got off the bus and started up the hill. Jess was a gymnast and I don't always cut games, so we were both pretty fit, but we had to stop halfway up because we'd been practically running.

I held my side and waited till I could breathe properly.

"Some people think they've got to talk to teenagers like that," I panted. "Take no notice."

"It made me feel . . . nasty."

I forced myself to look at her. For two pins she'd have cried.

"He's probably got a couple of kids at home and doesn't even smoke or drink."

"Yes." She took a deep breath. "I expect so."

It was half past two when we walked up the drive at Underwood. There were lots of trees around the house and it smelled like the country, damp and clean; the pollution hadn't got this far. They were very welcoming. A gray-haired woman answered the door and said we were expected and took us across polished tiles to the Head's room. His name was Mr. Bartlett and he was short and round with a shiny bald head. He was on his knees when we went in, looking at a wheelchair. The occupant of the chair, a girl about twelve, grinned down at his bald patch, and another bloke in a dark green overall stood by looking doubtful.

Bartlett looked over his shoulder at us and told us to take a pew for a minute. Then he spoke to the other bloke.

"You see, Joe, all it needs is a lever arrangement here." He jabbed his finger under the footrest.

"It would need a lot of strength to pull it, sir. You're asking the kids to lift the weight of their own legs."

Bartlett stood up. He really was short.

"Let's show him, Liz," he said.

The girl gave a little giggle, then wrapped her arms round his neck and lifted herself out of the chair. Her legs dangled uselessly as she took the weight of her whole body on her arms. Bartlett, rocklike under her body, let

36

her stay for a moment; then he lifted her carefully back into the chair.

"See, Joe?" He turned to us. "I'm trying to get our carpenter here to fix the kind of footrest the kids can adjust themselves. If the legs are constantly changing levels, it helps circulation. See what I mean?" I just nodded, but Bartlett grinned at Jess. "I can see I've got a convert in you, young lady." I looked at her. No blush. Her mouth was half open and she was the picture of keenness. "You agree with me, eh?"

"Well, Liz could manage it all right, couldn't she?"

Blimey, she'd already "related" to one of the kids.

This girl—Liz—immediately bowled forward and showed off her biceps.

Jess went right on, as if she could chat anyone up.

"What do *you* thing about it, Liz? Would you like to be able to make your legs go up and down?"

Liz made a garbled sound and nodded violently. I realized she had a speech handicap, as well as everything else, and thought it would crease Jess. Not a bit of it. She kept right on smiling and looking keen.

Bartlett was pleased right enough.

"Why don't you take your new friend through to the workroom, Liz?" he suggested. "And perhaps she'll tell you her name."

Jess has stood up, but at that she squatted by the wheelchair so that her head was on a level with the girl's.

"I'm Jessamy," she said gravely. "And I'd like to be your friend, Liz."

The girl made three distinct sounds through her nose

37

in imitation of the three syllables of *Jessamy*. I hadn't realized that was Jess's name myself and somehow I wanted to repeat it, too. I liked three-syllable names for girls, I decided. Except Margaret.

Jess went out behind the wheelchair and I stood up feeling a bit peculiar. Bartlett came just past my shoulder.

The other bloke, Joe, said, "Well, I'll do my best, Mr. Bartlett, but I can't guarantee nothing. I ain't got no magic wand, you know."

"Just a magic screwdriver, Joe." Bartlett grinned at him companionably and with complete trust. "I know you'll improvise something."

Joe went out, muttering something about a snow job. Bartlett perched on the edge of his desk and looked up at me.

"So you're interested in why we do this job, David?"

My God, Ruskin had done *her* job all right.

"Sort of, sir."

He laughed at my caution.

"I doubt if many of us will be able to tell you. We're not given to much self-analysis. But you can pop in any time if you're willing to make yourself useful. Talk to the kids and to us. We'd like to know what you make of us, and Miss Ruskin says if it's all right with you I can read your report later."

"That's all right with me." No one had ever asked my permission about that kind of thing before. I handed in a piece of work and it could be toted all over the world, for all I knew. Ruskin was a good sort. And Bartlett didn't seem bad either, except for this damned eagerness.

He took me over to this workroom place after that. It

was a big room with skylights and glass doors at the end leading into a paved garden. Along the walls, at waist height, were bookshelves. There was a loom. Painting easels. Low tables scattered with paper and cardboard, paste and scissors. Somewhere out of sight a typewriter tapped very sporadically.

The gray-haired woman who'd let us in came forward.

"Ah. Mrs. Preston. Is Jessamy all right?" Bartlett craned his neck to look over the easels.

"Liz is showing her the garden—it's not raining." Mrs P. looked at me without a smile. "And our other visitor wants to meet the children?"

"Yes, please. This is David." His voice rose on my name, and two or three heads looked up from their work. The already familiar grins broke out. "He'll give anyone a hand—"

He got no further. I thought the welcoming grins had been for Bartlett but they were for me, too. It was like being a pop star; I was surrounded and besieged.

After a lot of fuss—laughter from Bartlett, dry admonitions from Preston and a lot of shouting from the kids—I found myself crouching on the floor doing some collage work. A winter frieze or something. There were three kids with me, all in overalls, all pretty mobile on the highly polished floor. I was dead worried in case they couldn't talk or something, but apart from their legs they seemed okay. We did the name bit straight off.

"I'm Bobbie. I'm twelve and a half. My dad's called David, like you. He works for the Council. Where does your dad work?"

"In Bristol. He's in an insurance office." I looked

39

round at their expectant faces. I was the only one doing any collage. "His name's Alan. And my mum's called Rita."

One of them—a girl, of course—said, "That's probably shortened from Marguerita. That's the name of a flower. I'm Gudrun, but everyone calls me Goodie."

She looked a goodie, too. The other one of the trio, also a girl, said her name was Maria and her mum had the most beautiful name in the world. Rosabel.

"Yes, but your dad always calls her Rosie," Gudrun said swiftly. "My mum's name is April."

"Does your dad call her Ape?" asked Bobbie. We all collapsed, even Goodie. They were exactly like the twelve-year-olds at school—or the fifteen-year-olds, come to that—except for their legs. We got down to work and the quips went back and forth, and I could see Preston thought I was a bad influence. Then one of the glass doors opened and Jess came in with Liz. They came over and watched us, and Liz made one of her strangled noises at Jess. Jess said "Okay," and she and Mrs. Preston lifted Liz onto the floor. Goodie passed her a bundle of tiny blue scraps of material.

"Over here behind this tree, Liz. For the sky."

That made six of us round the frieze, so I sat back on my heels and took a rest. There was a lot going on in that room, most of it directed toward Christmas. Kids smiled across at me and held up their work for me to see. Paper angels, miniature Christmas trees, sleigh bells made from bottle tops. Except that the atmosphere was more relaxed, it was just like an ordinary school round about this time. Nothing to be embarrassed about.

Then Mrs. Preston came up. She was the sort who made you feel guilty for sitting doing nothing, but it was Jess she wanted to see, not me.

"I wondered . . . Have you had any typing lessons at your school, dear?" She bent over Jess's pale hair confidentially, one woman to another. I realized Jess was already part of the setup. She fitted in. I hadn't seen her go red once since we got here.

"Sorry, no." She looked around for me. "David. You took a typing option, didn't you?"

I'd done it for a pipe course. A real old biddy with a bun taught typing and she let you type out your homework or letters or anything. Naturally, like everything else, it ended up with the boys servicing the machines for the girls.

"Yes. I can't type, though. . . ." I didn't know Jess had a clue about my timetable.

Mrs. Preston actually managed a smile in my general direction. "Could you possibly give me a hand, David? The carriage of our machine seems to be stuck." She walked off, so I had to follow. I tried making a face at Jess, and she still didn't blush. In fact, she smiled and sort of shook her head at me.

We went past the loom and through a big sliding door into a kind of lean-to made of acrylic and full of potted plants. A boy sat in a wheelchair in the middle of a big open space. I realized straightaway he was spastic. The typewriter sat on a table near him looking lopsided. All that had happened was the carriage had slipped off one end. I released it and slid it back into position. As I did so, I read the paper in it. There was just one sentence, and it was hard to fathom because of the odd spacing and all the mistakes. It said, "On Saturday we did our dancing at the Albert Rooms."

"Gosh. Thanks very much."

The boy's chair came spinning crazily toward me and I only just got out of the way. He laughed without apology, and before he'd properly stopped he made a wild dab at the typewriter. He hit a T.

"Good. I want to say 'There were lots of people watching us.' Does that sound all right for the *Evening News*?"

"Sure. I saw the show. It was very good."

That sent him wild. His arms flew in all directions and he started to dribble. Mrs. Preston held him still and said sternly, "Swallow, Bruce. Go on, swallow." He swallowed convulsively and grinned without embarrassment.

"You can help me write it up then. I'm the press officer because I'm going to be a journalist. Will you help?"

"Sure." I said again. What else could I say? Mrs. Preston nodded, apparently happy, and wandered off. I felt scared.

The boy—Bruce—said, "I'll put that—'There were lots of people watching'—shall I?"

"Sure. I mean—yes. You do that."

He made a run at the table and missed it by miles. One arm shot up and caught me under the chin. He was breathless with laughter.

"Could you get me in close? . . . That's right. I need an H, don't I? I can spell all right—" He dabbed at the keyboard and got an M.

I said, "Try it with the other hand. I'll hold this one down. That is—if you don't mind."

"No. I don't mind. We're always trying different ways.

42

Bart says you've got to keep a completely open mind in this business."

Where had I heard that before? Ruskin had said something like it last Thursday; and Dad had used those very words, surely? Of course, he'd doubtless had them from his darling Maggie. It was the first time I'd thought of her for about an hour, and it wasn't nice. Like heartburn.

In the end I knelt down and put my arms tight round Bruce and the wheelchair, pinning him into it and keeping his right arm braced against my chest. Waveringly he reached out and tapped an H with his left hand.

"Hey! It worked." I let him go and he flailed about uncontrollably. "Quick—grab me again!" he yelled. So I did and after I'd edged the chair back to the table, he got an E. Only five minutes later he'd bashed out the word "There."

I was exhausted.

"How long have you been at this article?" I panted.

He thought about it.

"I started this morning about half past nine. Then I stopped for a cuppa. Then again for dinner—"

"You've stuck at it all day?" I said incredulously.

" 'Fraid so." He wasn't crestfallen. "I'm quicker when Mrs. Preston can spare the time to hang on to me."

I couldn't get over it. I didn't know anyone could have that much patience. We did another two words; then Jess came to say we'd have to go because it was four o'clock. I was getting to like old Bruce, too. There was something about him reminded me of Buff Harkins. He was easy. Nothing struck him as queer or odd. He flapped around in his chair in much the same way as Buff appeared at school in his awful batik shirts. As if to say: Well, this is me and you'll have to lump it.

I found a couple of bricks on the slatted shelves that held the potted plants, and I wedged the wheelchair with them so it wouldn't move from the table. There was a brake, but Bruce flipped that off automatically every time he started his tic-tac stuff. Then I took off my belt and strapped his right arm to his side.

"I'll be back for that," I warned him. "So don't lose it, else I'll have to spend the rest of my life with my hands in my pockets."

He flopped about laughing.

"When?" he said. I knew what he meant. But it was Jess who answered him.

"Wednesday," she said. "Miss Ruskin thought Monday, Wednesday and Friday afternoons till Christmas."

"Great," Bruce said.

Bartlett was outside in the drive helping load some of the kids into a minibus thing. Between us, Jess and me pushed a couple of wheelchairs up the ramp. You had to be strong to work in this place; of course Jess was a good gymnast but she'd need to be fit if she took that job next summer.

"What happens to Bruce?" I asked Bartlett as we said our thank-yous and good-byes. "Does he live here?"

Bartlett shook his head. "We're not a residential school. The children here all have happy homes. Bruce is fourteen; he will wait for the next trip." He looked up at me. Already I was forgetting his Charlie Chaplin impression. He might be short but he was a powerful bloke, like one of those short-legged bulls. He said, "Bruce is all right."

"Yes." I thought about it. "Yes, he is."

"I'm glad you've latched onto him. Some young people—old ones, too—are all uptight about spastics when they meet them in the flesh."

I felt guilty remembering how scared I'd been to find myself alone with Bruce. He turned to Jess then and talked to her about Goodie and Maria. She seemed to know most of the kids by name and kept asking intelligent questions.

Then he said, "Well I must be going—we'll hope to see you on Wednesday afternoon. You should be in time to help finish that Bruce Daly article."

He waved cheerfully and went back into the hall, and Jess and me plodded off down the drive to meet the smell of car exhausts coming up from the city. It all seemed strangely inevitable. I was hardly surprised. I'd gone to find out something about Margaret Daly and I'd found out she had a son nearly my age. Handicapped.

Well. That was what I'd wanted, wasn't it?

I couldn't think why I wanted to rush away from Jess and dash into the Cathedral and have a good cry in one of the side chapels.

I must be going soft in the head or something.

6

That week went quicker than most. On Wednesday we went to Underwood again and this time we were old friends. Jess took Liz for a walk and I hung on to Bruce while he finished his article. Yes, it had taken him three days to type out a single paragraph. And he wasn't fed up or bored, just elated.

There was a carol practice that day in their assembly hall, and afterward Bruce read out his news item and everyone clapped for him. He swung his arms wildly and started to dribble, and I pinioned his arms and said out of the side of my mouth, "For Pete's sake, swallow that blasted spit!"

I felt great when he did.

Going home in the bus, I told Jess about it.

"He's got to *tell* himself to do things—and then it doesn't always work. I mean . . . if we want to use the typewriter our hands go automatically to it. He has to keep saying, 'Hand—to typewriter!' It sounds daft but it's true. If he can't manage it, someone else can help by telling him. Like I did with the spit."

Surprisingly, Jess nodded immediately. "Yes, I know. That's how it is when I'm on the bar sometimes. I stand there ready to do a turn and my brain says it's impossible. Then Mrs. Wedmore yells out, 'Right foot swing—left foot twist—and turn,' and I just do it."

I looked at her. "Is it that difficult?"

"Yes." She gave a little laugh. "I only do it because I'm too scared not to!"

I said slowly, "No. You're brave. You and Bruce. You're both brave." It sounded so sloppy. I was quite glad when she went red and clammed up.

On Thursday it poured rain, and Games were called off. We were herded into the library for a quiet study

46

hour, and as soon as poss I cleared off down to the gym and watched through the glass doors as the girls did their floor work. Jess didn't look scared. She looked terrific. Her colorless hair was scraped back into an elastic band and her face looked small and very serious as she twisted herself into fantastic shapes on the floor. I suddenly realized she wasn't using her legs. Jess was working out a floor sequence that maybe Liz and Bobbie and Gudrun could use.

On Friday she and Bruce had quite a chat. She told him what she had told me, about forcing her limbs to work when they didn't always want to.

Bruce said, as if it was a big laugh, "Your arms obey you. Mine don't."

"I'm always surprised when mine do," Jess said, laughing with him. "I never believe I can do it. Mrs. Wedmore says one day I'll learn confidence. But I haven't yet."

I said, thinking it out as I went along, "It's kind of matter over mind, isn't it? Your mind doesn't believe your body can do these things, so your body has to—well, prove it, I suppose."

Bruce said tentatively, "Since Monday . . . I've thought my left arm was more . . . obedient."

We exchanged glances wondering if we were onto something. Bruce said over the weekend he would practice drawing with his left hand and let us know how he got on when he saw us Monday. He grinned. "I suppose if I manage something good, you two will want all the credit."

He had a way of taking the tension out of things, making them relaxed and easy. Like Buff.

I was dreading seeing Dad on Saturday. I hadn't said a word to Mum about Bruce; just told her I was visiting Underwood for my Environmental Studies project and left it at that. She didn't know Margaret Daly worked there; in fact we hadn't mentioned Dad since last week.

But if I told Dad, he'd know I had some special reasons for going there. In some ways, Dad had a nasty suspicious nature. I decided to keep quiet.

He arrived early and, I'm glad to say, found me cleaning the windows. Mum had offered me fifty pence four weeks ago if I'd do the outsides and I was just getting round to it.

Dad told me to keep going and watched me from the front gate.

"You're better then?"

For a minute I forgot I'd been on the point of puking up when I saw him last. Though the week had gone so quickly, it still seemed years since that awful bus ride back home from the Albert Rooms.

"Eh? Oh, yeah. Remind me to keep off Italian food in future."

I concentrated on getting into the corner of the pane, but I knew Dad wouldn't let me get away with anything like Mum would. Then a bloke up the road went past on his bike and didn't know whether to speak to Dad or not, so Dad went on in and said he'd make us a cup of coffee. He doesn't care about that sort of thing, but he thinks it's bad for me. I suppose he hasn't noticed I cut out speaking to anyone over a year ago. It's simpler that way.

I did the rest of the windows and went in, and Dad sent me up to Cooky's for some doughnuts and we sat and gorged blissfully. Dad asked if I was really all right now. Then was Mum all right, and had the chap come to clean out the guttering on the house. I said yes, yes, yes. Then I asked after Gran and Gramps and Uncle Phil and the insurance business. He said Gran wanted me to go there for Christmas.

"Phil's got a new girl. She's having his room and he's sleeping on the sofa. I thought the four of us could get out of Gran's way and go to the carols at the Cathedral. Then Boxing Day we could try skating again. D'you remember when we went before and Phil tried to go backward?"

"Mum was with us then."

I hated him at that moment. Did he think I could spend Christmas living it up at Gran's and leave Mum here? Yet I remembered the city last Saturday and the Christmassy smell of it all, and I wanted desperately to go.

He resorted to his monosyllable.

"Yes."

It made me hate him worse. No excuses, no apologies.

So I said as nastily as I dared, "Why don't you ask Mrs. Daly to spend Christmas at Gran's with you?"

There was a horrible silence. I stared stubbornly out the window at the net of nuts Mum had pegged on the line for the birds. It's funny how rows spring up out of nothing. A couple of minutes ago, we'd been all over sugar from the doughnuts, talking about things that didn't matter. And now here was something that did matter and we were hating each other. I wondered if this was how it had been with Mum and Dad.

At last he said, "So that's what it's all about."

That made me angrier than ever. I didn't know if that was what it was all about or not, but it sounded a bit too simple, too easy to be the right answer. Teenage boy, jealous of prospective stepmother? Not on your nelly.

I tried to imitate Jasper's insulting voice as I said, "You should know, Dad. You're the one with all the answers."

But he refused to lose his temper. "Not quite, Dave. For instance, I'm not at all sure that Mrs. Daly would want to spend Christmas with me."

There's a poem by Keats or Wordsworth or someone that starts "My heart leapt up." I put it down to poetic license before, but no, it's for real, because my heart leapt up when Dad said that. It meant things hadn't gone as far as I'd imagined—not that I'd dared to imagine much. I'd shut Daly up at the back of my mind and I didn't even think of her when I was with Bruce. In fact, it often came as a shock to realize she was Bruce's mother.

I didn't say anything. My mind was wondering how I could use this uncertainty to finish off the whole thing.

Dad said quietly, "Margaret Daly and I are friends, Dave. Nothing more." That phrase . . . "just good friends" . . . Besides, hadn't I watched Dad's face at the Albert Rooms? He went on, making it worse all the time, "I admire her more than I can say. Devoting her life to those poor kids—" Well, at least he hadn't called them paraplegics, but that was what he meant. Not Bobbie, Goodie, Maria, Liz, but "those poor kids." And suddenly I thought I knew the answer. Dad didn't know about Bruce. He thought Daly was some sort of saint.

I said roughly, "I think I'm going to throw up."

50

"What d'you mean?"

"Just good friends . . . admire her more than you can say . . . devote her life . . . oh, my God. She does it for her own sake, Dad. Probably gets reduced fees or something. She's got a spastic son at Underwood's. He's nearly as old as me and he can't do a thing for himself!"

There was another ghastly silence, but I wasn't worrying about Dad anymore. I couldn't think why but I felt terrible. I really did want to puke up.

Dad said slowly, "Did you think I didn't know about Bruce? Maggie told me about him the first time we met. We toss up for who can have first go at talking about their son. She's as proud of him as I am of you."

I felt really ill but I couldn't leave it alone.

"Have you met him?"

"No. Not yet."

"I have. He can't control his arms at all. And he dribbles."

"Maggie tells me he thinks the world of you."

It came to me then that Dad had known all along that I'd been to Underwood's. He'd talked about it with "Maggie." And he couldn't have said a thing that would cut my anger off so abruptly. This whole thing between Dad and me was still enormous . . . horrible . . . but there was something else now.

I said desperately, "Does Bruce know who I am? Does he know about you? Does he know I'm your son?" I couldn't bear the thought that Bruce might guess my visits had been sort of . . . spying.

"No. I told you. I haven't met Bruce yet."

"But Mrs. Daly might have said something—"

"Bruce went on and on about his friend David. So Maggie asked the Head who David was. She thought it was the most marvelous coincidence that you should have got to know her son. I'm a bit more cynical and I wondered. Now I know, don't I?"

"Listen, Dad—" It was such a relief to know that Bruce didn't suspect me I forgot for a minute that I hated Dad. "Listen. I went there to find out about your Mrs. Daly— all right, I admit that. But I met Bruce by chance—he messed up his typewriter and they asked me to see to it. It wasn't till we were leaving I found out he was Mrs. Daly's son. That's the truth. Honest."

"My God . . ." Dad was looking at me as if he'd never seen me before. It must have seemed like a big intrigue hearing it all at once like that. "And Maggie thought we'd let you both get all palsy-walsy and then spring it on you that your parents were friends, too! What's happened to you, Dave?"

That hurt. It hurt most because he didn't *know*. Mum had known instantly. She had felt as I felt, too, yet she'd understood Dad's point of view. But Dad didn't seem to be able to see anything from our angle anymore. I looked at him and he was just the same as when he'd lived with us. Fair, sandy-dry hair, gray eyes—hard now, like pebbles—that long pugnacious jaw. He was wearing flannels and a bulky sweater, so probably we hadn't been going to tea with Mrs. Daly. . . . Well, we certainly wouldn't be now.

I felt like saying "What's happened to *you*?" But I didn't. It was getting like those confrontations with Eccles and the other teachers—even Miss Ruskin, up till last week—when my only bet was to clam right up or stick to the monosyllables. Dad was with *them* now. On the other side of the great chasm that separated most kids from most adults.

In the end, I just got up and walked over to the window and looked out and didn't see even the bird food on the clothesline.

Dad waited a bit; then he said, "I thought of going over the Mendip Hills. We could talk this out."

I still didn't say anything. What was there to talk out? I'd done what I'd done. I'd probably do it again if I thought there was a chance of ousting Daly from Dad's life. If Dad found it all so awful, then that's what he'd have to go on feeling.

He tried again. "Would you like to do that? Drive up Burrington Coombe and over the top to Wells?"

A watery slice of sun lit up the garden. It would be nice on the hills, wintry and quiet. But all I could see was a smear on the window where I'd missed with the polishing rag.

Dad said woodenly, "At least have the courtesy to answer me, Dave. Do you want to go for a drive?"

"No."

"Do you want to talk? Here?"

"No."

"Right then." He came and stood by me. I wouldn't look at him. "I ought to whack you, Dave. But you're past whacking. Perhaps you don't need it." He shoved his hands into his trouser pockets as if he didn't trust them. "Think over what you've just told me, son. Perhaps we can talk about it again when I come next week."

"Don't bother," I managed.

53

I must have sounded pretty poisonous, because that seemed to shake him. He said in a low voice, "I won't come unless you ring me then. You've got Gran's number." He hung about a bit more; then he said, "I'll go, Dave."

I said, "Cheerio."

He shut the front door carefully and I didn't hear him drive away.

I counted about forty to make sure he was really gone; then I went up to the bathroom and sat on the seat with a comic. But I didn't read it. I said out loud, "I'm sorry, Bruce."

Then I screwed the comic up tight and shut my eyes hard and swore. Over and over again I swore. And I still didn't feel any better.

7

That night and all day Sunday, I stuck to Mum like I was a little kid again, and by Monday morning I was able to convince myself nothing was wrong. I would just stop thinking about Dad and his Daly woman and Bruce and they wouldn't exist. I sort of put a Berlin Wall across the Bristol road somewhere, and they were one side and I was the other.

Course, I didn't tell her a thing. Just that Dad had had some business on Saturday and couldn't stop. She was dead pleased about the windows and the furniture—I polished that all afternoon—and on Sunday we went for a walk up the woods and came back with holly and ivy for Christmas decorations. She said it reminded her of when she was a girl. She nearly said it reminded her of old times, but she changed it in time. Other kids' mums have this embarrassing habit of talking about them when they were in diapers and bringing out those old snapshots. Mum doesn't because that usually means mentioning Dad. Sometimes I think I was born when I was twelve years old, because the last three years is all the past that we talk about. But it's all right to talk about the time before I was around, so she told me about how she and her sisters used to decorate the church hall for the pantomime the air-raid wardens used to put on. If it hadn't been for her father getting killed, Mum would have enjoyed the war a lot.

On Monday the Art woman told Jess and me we could go over to the Sixth Form block and help paint the flats for *The Mikado*. Miss Ruskin had evidently had a word with Marilyn and Jock and that lot, because we were in a little corner on our own with her, filling in outlines on hardboard with dark blue paint. She said when it was finished it would look like a bridge over a lily pond. The set was taken from a willow-pattern plate thing, all blue and white. Jess said it sounded marvelous, then went deep red and shut up.

Anyway, Miss Ruskin asked us about Underwood and how it was going and all, and Jess gradually opened up and between us we put her in the picture. I felt a bit of a louse as I'd no intention of showing my face there again, but I didn't want to tell them in advance because that would mean an explanation. If I just didn't turn up, all I'd have to do would be shrug, or say I got fed up, and there'd be nothing they could do about it.

I couldn't quite leave it like that, though. I knew Jess would have kittens all the way to Bristol on the bus thinking I'd missed it or got myself run over or something. So I went along to the bus stop at one-thirty and told her I was packing it in.

"Oh, David." She looked so disappointed and she forgot to blush even. She didn't say anything stupid like "Why?" Just "Oh, David."

"Yeah." I let my left foot dangle off the curb into the running gutter. My sock felt clammy cold so there must be a hole in my shoe. The bus came round the corner.

"You won't change your mind?"

"No."

I watched her stand on the step and get her fare and find a seat. She looked forlorn. I hoped no smart-aleck driver would make any snide remarks to her and make her run up Church Road. She didn't look at me till the bus started to draw out; then she glanced up quick, saw me staring at her and went bright red. But she managed to wave as well. I was glad about that.

She must have given me a decent cover, because nothing was said till Thursday afternoon.

I'd managed to get my name down for swimming, which meant every Games period was given over to practice in the pool. I'd done a couple of dozen lengths and surfaced to grin into Jasper's ugly face in the lane next to me, when I spotted Miss Ruskin hovering by the foot-

56

bath. I knew this was it. When I got to the shallow end, she was waiting for me.

"In my room at the end of school, please, David" was all she said. She didn't even wait to see if I'd heard, which I might not have seeing my ears were full up. She knew I'd be there. And I was.

"I'm sorry to hear about the sinus trouble, David," she said, not bothering to sit at the coffee table so it must be going to be a quickie. I looked blank for a moment. Sinus trouble? Then I realized Jess had been at work. Good old Jess. She was a classy liar when she had to be, but I was willing to lay a bet she'd gone as red as a turkey-cock when she told that one.

I grunted and sort of shrugged and tried to look brave.

"Are you sure swimming won't make it worse?"

Ruskin looked me straight between the eyes, and I let my gaze slide down to her face and ankles. Nice ankles. Mum sets great store by a woman's ankles.

"Dunno," I said like a yob.

She sighed and turned away and fiddled with her case.

"Are you going to Underwood tomorrow?" she asked without expression.

I didn't think she'd start badgering me for explanations but I couldn't be certain, so I shrugged again.

"Probably," I said.

She knew as well as I did that I wouldn't go. But she left it at that.

"Right. You can help with the *Mikado* sets again, if you like, on Monday. Tell me all about it. Good-bye then, David."

"Good-bye, Miss."

I drifted out and she didn't come with me. I'd have to get out of Monday morning painting now, which was a pity because I enjoyed it. Things had seemed as if they were opening out a bit; now they were closing in tighter than before.

I made for the Common room thinking I'd find Jess and say thanks for the lie, but Jasper's hairy hand came out of the shower room and pulled me inside as I passed. He was still messing about in his swimming trunks and his towel was a soggy dripping lump on the floor.

I twisted free. "Gerroff. You're soaking," I told him frigidly.

"Nemmind that. Listen, Wint. We want you to have a word with Buff. He listens to you. Get yourself invited out to his place to tea or something, make a good impression—"

"Who's we?" I asked. I'd seen he was badgering Buff all week about the North Devon trip. He wasn't that keen himself, but he enjoyed putting Buff into a tricky position.

"Rorie and me, you nutter. We were all invited to go to Woolacombe or wherever Jem's crazy cottage is, right? Now he's backing out, the little runt."

"Act your age Jas." I saw Buff come out from the canvas curtain. His clothes were soaked, and either he'd been crying or the chlorine in the water made his eyes swell. "Buff's parents aren't going to let us lot go down there, are they? Probably Jem put his foot down straightaway. It's his cottage."

"Buff said . . ." Jasper repeated stubbornly. He went on and on. Same old thing, over and over again. Rorie

58

joined us; he was pretty wet, too. I began to be thankful I'd had to pop off to see Ruskin and missed the party.

"I'm not keen myself," I told them. Then shut up till they'd finished their chorus of "Rotten swine . . . crying off . . . Mummy's boy . . ." "But"—I looked over their heads with a long-suffering face—"I will do my utmost on your behalf."

They liked that sort of talk and snuffled around like a couple of dogs straight out of the river, butting me with their wet heads and imagining they were a pair of Cass Clays. I made sure one of my answering jabs landed Rorie on his backside; then I sheered off. But there was no sign of Jess or Buff Harkins. Mart Coles was writing up his notes for a debate we were having tomorrow on euthanasia, and I wondered whether Buff had mentioned the Devon trip to him yet. He'd be okay with old Buff. He might even enjoy himself, for once.

Then I got myself down to the bike sheds and off to the paper round. I'd been doing it early all week so I could watch telly with Mum when she got in. Last night I persuaded her to have a hand of cribbage. She kept saying eight and six added up to fifteen, and in the end we were laughing too much to peg up our scores properly.

But nothing had stayed still since Dad took me to the Albert Rooms on the fifteenth. After our bust-up last Saturday, I'd tried to push everything away from Mum and me, protect us in a little space of our own, but I couldn't.

It was that night, the Thursday, she told me about going into the hospital.

She led into it so gently I didn't have a clue. I'd actually made the tea and was cutting bread and butter when she got in. It was raining but not hard, and she'd managed just with an umbrella. She stood in the kitchen door twirling it outside so that drops flew in all directions. Her short curly hair was haloed with droplets, too, and she'd put a plastic bag over her basket to keep the shopping dry, and that was a misty silver. It was practically dark but I hadn't put the lights on, and she was surprised to see me at the kitchen table hacking away in the gloaming.

She said, "I thought you must be watching the news. It's so dark out here."

"Nice, though. Christmassy." A minute ago I'd been humming "Once in Royal David's City" in an effort to conjure up Christmas right here, and not just in Bristol with Uncle Phil and his new girl friend and the skating rink all crowded and freezing.

"Crazy boy," she commented, and went into the hall to hang up her mack. "Had a good day? How's your Miss Ruskin?"

"She's got nice ankles. But I think she might be going off me."

"Never." Mum came in and switched on the light. She was flushed and her eyes were very bright before she blinked. "How could anyone go off a tall handsome lad like you? Here, I'll go on with that. There's steak pies in my bag—they're hot, so watch it—" She clattered round getting us organized. It was a lovely tea. I had eight pieces of bread and butter, and sauce with my pie, four cups of tea and three bananas. Nothing puts me off my food.

Mum sat there watching me and grinning a bit; then she said, "Talking of Christmas. I've been thinking you ought to spend it with Dad this year. It would liven it up a bit for Gran and Gramps now that Phil's moved out."

"He'll be home for Christmas," I said quickly. "And I think Dad said he was taking his girl friend, too."

Normally Mum would kibosh the idea straightaway with a comment about not putting them out, but tonight she said, "Well, that won't stop you going, love. Gran used to have that bed-settee in the front room—Phil can have that. It'll be fun for you."

If only it hadn't been for Daly I could have gone; Mum was handing it to me on a plate. Though the thought of her here on Christmas Day with just the telly and the afternoon tea party at the nursing home was a bit much.

"I'd rather stay here with you, Mum. There'll be more to eat."

She grinned obediently but her thoughts were elsewhere.

"I ought to stay at home on Saturday and have a word with your father," she said half to herself, causing my heart to bounce a bit.

"He's not coming—I meant to tell you. I'm going into Bristol to meet him. The eleven-o'clock bus." Those sort of touches give a lie substance. Like Jess saying I'd got sinus trouble instead of just any old cold. You find you believe it yourself.

Surprisingly Mum said, "Damn," as if she really did want to see Dad. Then she went on, "Still, it's probably better to leave it to you to fix it up. Then I can write a

61

letter to Gran thanking her, and it won't make a big thing out of it."

She couldn't have heard what I said. I put on an orphan face. "You're trying to get rid of me, aren't you?"

"Just for Christmas, love." She seemed to be pleading. "The house is here, and I know you'll keep it going all right the rest of the time. But Christmas itself—I want you to go to Dad."

I couldn't think straight. I knew one thing for certain, though: I couldn't go to Dad's. I stared at Mum across the table and noticed silly things like her hair going gray and her earlobes, both very bright red.

She smiled brightly. "It's nothing to worry about these days. And it could prevent something serious later on. I wish the bed hadn't come up just at Christmas, but still that's how it goes. I go in tomorrow week. That's the fifth of December, isn't it?" She got up and went to the calendar hanging by the electric fire. She flapped a page up and ran her finger down the numbers. I knew she couldn't see them.

"You're going into the hospital?" I said in my best two-tone voice. My throat had gone completely dry. "You never said anything. What for? Why didn't you tell me?"

She gave up looking at the calendar. "Well, you know what these waiting lists are like, Dave. No need to jump the gun. It could have been a year or more."

"But it's next week?"

"There's a free bed, you see. A cancellation or something."

"It must be serious if they're pushing you in so soon. What is it?"

"Of course it's not serious. An operation—quite commonplace these days. They simply remove something I've no use for anymore—"

"A hysterectomy."

"Well . . . yes."

"I am fifteen, you know. And I've been doing human biology for over three years now."

"Okay. A hysterectomy. But I don't want you thinking I've got something wrong. It's a preventive measure. That's all."

I didn't say anything. I was shivering. Mum being cut open by some man in a white mask . . . inhuman beings who wouldn't know or care anything about her. I got up and went over to the fire and crouched by it.

Mum said briskly, "Yes, it is better this way, Dave. Fix up about Christmas, but don't tell your father about the operation. He'd worry about you and the house— you know what he's like. Besides . . . he might feel he ought to come and see me. And I don't want that. Okay?"

I nodded. Christmas didn't matter anymore. Nothing did.

"Where . . . where will it be? Where are you going?"

"Bristol. Just for a week. Then I'll be at the cottage hospital to convalesce. I shall be quite okay then, but they won't let me home until the New Year. At least that's what Mathieson says at the moment. We'll see." Mathieson was our doctor. He was a good bloke.

"You ought to have told me."

"Whatever for? There was nothing to tell you till now. . . . Is there any more tea in the pot?"

I got up and poured her a cup. Poor old Mum. If she'd

had a daughter, she could have talked it all out. If she'd had Jess. Yes, Jess would have listened and told her not to worry, everything would be all right.

I said, "Don't worry, Mum, will you? Everything will be all right."

And she said in that same brisk tone, "Of course it will, love. So long as I know you're fixed up with Gran over the school holidays, I shan't worry about a thing."

"It'll be a nice rest," I said, trying a shaky grin.

And she actually managed a laugh. "It certainly will," she said.

8

I couldn't face school the next day; well, not so much school as the people in it. The thought of Mart Coles going on about euthanasia being the only solution to our crippling tax burden made me feel really ill. Mart Coles is the sort who talks about old people and spastics as "them," never "us."

So after Mum had gone I locked up and sat around for a couple of hours telling myself how great it was to be missing school. Then I rang up old Mathieson's surgery and asked to speak to him. The woman on the other end said he was just going out on his rounds, and who was it. I said David Winterbourne and it didn't matter, I'd ring again another time. Next thing Mathieson's voice nearly blew my ear out.

"David? Want to talk about your mother, do you? Look, I've got a house call down your road. I'll pop in."

"The neighbors will wonder what—"

"Sod the neighbors. If they say anything to your mother, tell her the truth. It'll do her good to know someone's worried about her welfare."

"Okay." I had to laugh. Like I said, Mathieson was a good bloke. He didn't say anything about me being at home instead of at school.

He arrived as I was opening a tin of beans.

"So you're worried? Any good me giving you a speech about the foolproof methods of modern surgery?"

I shook my head. Seeing him sitting on the kitchen stool had a funny effect on me; I wanted to cry. It ought to be Dad sitting there. And it could be . . . it would have been if we hadn't had that row, because whatever Mum said I would have telephoned him at work that morning and I knew he'd have come straight over.

"Well, then I won't say it." He picked up a piece of my toast and took a bite. "All that part is taken for granted, okay? All I need tell you is that there is at present no malignancy inside your mother. She's coming up to forty and she had a routine smear test. Are you with me?"

I nodded. I had given up the beans and was staring at him as if I could will the absolute truth out of him.

"The test revealed that maybe—in another six or seven years or so—she might have trouble." He swallowed the toast and looked back at me steadily. "A growth in her womb."

Somehow or other I swallowed, too. Then I said, "I see."

"So the obvious thing to do is to remove the womb. That is why we do these tests. Saves no end of trouble in the future." He tore off a bit more toast.

"Yes." I couldn't think of anything else to say, but luckily Mathieson knew the sort of questions that would occur to me later.

"It's one of the bigger operations, of course, but done now it's absolutely straightforward. However, I knew your mother would worry about it, so when this bed became vacant I suggested she take it." He munched judiciously. "And I thought it might be easier for you over Christmas, too, old man."

"Me? How?"

"Your father and you should be together at such a time. It might have been difficult during termtime."

"Oh . . . yes."

"They won't mind you breaking up a bit early, will they? You can go in with your mother next Friday and then straight to your grandmother's. You can visit her on Saturday and Sunday; then they'll probably keep you at arms' length till the Wednesday. Probably over the actual holiday weekend she'll be back here in the cottage hospital, but your father can bring you over, can't he?"

I kept nodding. Mum must have let him think I would be spending all the school holidays with Dad, but she hadn't mentioned it to me. We'd never talked about Margaret Daly again, but I had a sudden feeling Margaret Daly was the reason Mum didn't want Dad to know about her operation. And the reason I wasn't being coerced into spending all my holidays with Dad.

Mathieson went on, "Would you like me to write a

note to your headmaster?"

I stopped nodding. "No, thanks. I'll explain. It'll be all right. A relief, probably. They don't know what to do with us this year. Till we're sixteen and can leave."

He laughed and changed the subject to school and what I was going to do afterward. I didn't tell him about the Army. Anyway, I didn't really know what I wanted to do anymore.

The next day, believe it or not, I caught the eleven-o'clock bus to Bristol. I had this daft feeling that if I didn't actually lie to Mum she'd be all right. I know it was crazy, but that was how I felt then. And I'd told her I was going to Bristol on the eleven-o'clock bus. So I went. I conveniently shut my mind to the fact that I'd told Mum I was catching the flipping bus in order to meet Dad. I'd no intention at all of seeing Dad; probably not until I was about twenty.

I got off at the center and looked at the neon news flashes and ads going along on top of the Hippodrome. After the second Haig whisky, I crossed over into the telephone boxes and rang Jasper. My twopence stuck for a minute in the slot, and Mrs. Ingham sounded panicky when all the clanking died away.

"Hello. Hello. Hello. Who is there, please? Will you speak up, please? I cannot hear you—"

"It's me, Mrs. Ingham. David. Is Jasper there?"

She made a noise of disgust and put the receiver down on something with a terrible clunk. I heard her ordinary voice, high and nasal, giving Jasper a hard time. "If you think we pay for that phone just so your friends can ring you up for a chat—he only lives five minutes away—lazy devils, the lot of you—" Then Jasper bawled, "Hi, Wint. Any progress to report?"

I'd been away a day, and he didn't even ask me what was wrong. He was practically an egomaniac.

"What sort of progress?" I bawled back vengefully.

"My God, Wint. You wanna watch that. You nearly burst my flaming eardrum—"

"What sort of progress?" I yelled again at the top of my voice.

"Okay, funnyman. Progress with Buff. The hippie trip, man. Like—uh—our little old Christmas vay-cation."

I caught at the words. Christmas vacation. A trip to North Devon over Christmas! Would Mum wear it? Was Buff persuadable? If—if—if—just *if* I could swing it, I could get out of the business with Dad so neat and nice . . . and honest, man.

"Could be," I said enigmatically like Humphrey Bogart. "Just could be, sweetheart. Would your folks be—like—agreeable?"

He said in a much lower voice, "Look. I got them where I want them, baby. How about yours?"

"I'm working on it. . . . Hey, Jas. How about getting on a bus and joining me in Broadmead? I've got two weeks' paper money on me. Treat you to fishcake and chips at Littlewoods."

"Then what?"

"Well. The museum's free. And there's the library and the Cathedral."

"Big deal. There's a match on telly at two."

"Thanks a bunch," I said bitterly.

68

"Why? You already there? Where's Daddy then?"

"Shut up."

But I couldn't poke him over the phone, so he went on a bit and I had to hang up. I immediately dialed again, shoved the twopence in as quick as I could and stood there breathing heavily into the mouthpiece.

Mrs. Ingham yelped. "My God! It's one of those anonymous breathers—hello—hello—say something!"

In the background Jasper said eagerly, "It's only old Wint. Give it to me, I'll worry him—" Then the phone went dead.

I wondered what to do next. Fishcake and chips didn't sound bad, so I wandered on to Broadmead, past the back of the hospital where this time next week Mum would be, and went straight into Littlewoods. It was all done up with Christmas stars and styrofoam reindeers and it was very bright and warm after the blowing drizzle outside. There was a counter labeled "Gift Suggestions Under £1," so I walked along it and tried to find something for Mum. Hot-water bottles, silk scarves, cheap jewelry, brush-and-comb sets, toilet bags. None of it special enough. I wanted something decent this year.

Then I saw Jess. I stood and watched her for ages. She was on her own, looking through the cheap jewelry tray. Her hair was wet and she'd pushed it behind her ears so that her face showed like it did when she was doing her floor work in the gym. She was wearing a nylon mack and it was undone; underneath it she had her school skirt and blazer on. I wondered whether her folks were very poor.

I'd made up my mind to follow her around a bit when

69

she looked up and saw me. This time she smiled *before* she went red, which I felt showed progress. I went over.

"None of it would suit you," I said as a greeting. "It's not classy enough."

I didn't mean it as a compliment but I suppose it was, and she looked startled, but she couldn't go any redder.

"It's for Liz. She'd like a charm bracelet but they're ever so expensive."

"Liz?"

"At Underwood."

"Oh, yes." Jess really was one of them, buying Christmas presents. And I couldn't go there again. I felt a definite sense of loss. "How are they all?"

"Just the same. Except Bruce. Something's different about him. Perhaps he misses you."

"Oh, shut up."

"No, I mean it. He's different. We get on well—he talks a lot about you. Then suddenly on Friday he went all moody."

"How d'you mean?" I wondered whether he'd met Dad—whether Dad had told him who I was. If he had, I thought I might hate Dad as much as I hated Margaret Daly.

"I don't know. His arms wouldn't stay still and he didn't show me his drawings like he had been doing. He said no wonder you didn't come anymore—"

"Why did he say that?"

"I suppose he thought he wasn't much fun or something. He's bound to get depressed now and then."

"But . . . it made him laugh. His mistakes—his arms going—it all made him laugh." I sounded a fool standing there by the jewelry counter repeating myself.

70

"Yes, but sometimes—it must get him down."

I let it drop, and fiddled around with a brooch shaped like an umbrella till an assistant asked if she could help me.

"No, thanks." I looked at Jess. "Fancy a cup of coffee?"

She didn't say yes but she didn't say no, either, so after a bit I shuffled toward the stairs and she stayed with me. I sat her at a table right over the top of the women's bras and fetched two coffees. The fishcakes looked lovely.

"My gran used to bring me here a lot," I said conversationally. "When she wasn't looking, I used to try and spit down into those medium cups."

"David! You're just saying that. I don't believe you." She was laughing, horrified and fascinated.

"True." I took a mouthful of coffee. "I'll do it again, if you like."

"Don't you dare! I'd die of embarrassment—" But the ice was broken and we started talking about when we were kids.

I remembered how Dad always took me to the museum to see the Bristol Box Kite. It's suspended from the ceiling about three floors up, and you can get to see it from about a million different angles. Even from the top floor, real close up, it looked like something modeled out of old matchsticks.

"I seriously considered jumping across to it and pretending I was flying it as it swung back and forth," I told Jess, filling my saucer with salt so I wouldn't have to look at her. "It would have been like those old films with Errol Flynn where he grabs a handy chandelier and

71

whips right over the room—"

"Or like Tarzan on one of those handy vine things. I love Tarzan. Just to think of him makes me want to leap for that big star over there and hurtle over the heads of all those busy women yelling and yodeling—"

I stared at her in amazement. She had blue eyes. I hadn't noticed that before.

"You could, too," I said. "I've seen you on a rope in the gym. You could do it."

"No. Not me." She laughed, a bit embarrassed but not curled up about it. "You might fly the Box Kite one day, though, David. You're the sort of person who could do something really mad and grand."

I thought of her in the gym; then I thought of her again kneeling down by that wheelchair saying "I'm Jessamy"; then again going red and miserable when that bus driver spoke to us. *She* hadn't asked me why I was away on Friday either, but only because she respected my privacy. A bit like Miss Ruskin.

We talked about other daft pretend games we'd had. We laughed a lot. Suddenly I found myself telling her about Mum going into the hospital and wanting to get her a decent Christmas present for once.

"Something that says Happy Christmas, and get well, and is special," she mused, eyeing the counters beneath us for inspiration. "You want something she can boast about in hospital. Parents enjoy boasting about their kids." Poor old Mum. She missed out on that, too. "How about a really nice bed jacket?" She didn't look very hopeful, but I thought about it and liked the idea. I could see Mum sitting up in bed wearing something very frilly—blue, I thought—and saying complacently, "Yes, my son bought it me for Christmas. It *is* rather nice, isn't it?"

"Are there any here?" I asked, craning over the balustrade and loving it when she gasped and told me to be careful.

She narrowed her eyes. "Ye-es. They're dear. One ninety-nine."

"I've got that much on me. But I haven't had anything to eat yet." I'd already planned to buy fishcake and chips for Jess in a minute.

"Don't worry about that. Let's get it while you've got the money. Then you've got it."

It was an irrefutable argument. We went back downstairs, and I must admit I felt better than I'd felt since last night when the girl wrapped it in tissue, then put it in a special Christmas carrier. Then we walked out into the cold again, and there was the Salvation Army playing carols in the drizzle. It was nice.

Jess said regretfully, "I'll have to go. I'm catching the train from Temple Meads and it's quite a walk."

"You're going home on the train?"

"I nearly always do. My granddad's a railwayman, so I get cheap tickets."

"I didn't know." Did she live with her grandparents then? "I'll walk along with you. I'm not in any hurry."

We tramped along the ring road and through the underpass and everyone looked smiley, especially when I started humming "Once in Royal David's City" in my cracked voice.

When we got to the approach, Jess said, "Can you

afford a platform ticket? Someone I know works in the refreshment room and she'll let us have any sandwiches or cakes that are stale. That is, if you're hungry."

I felt as if she'd invited me to a banquet. It was years since I'd been in the station.

It was the buffet on Platform 5. The lady in there must have weighed about two hundred fifty and you didn't notice anything about her face except her smile. She was a wonderful advertisement for the food and atmosphere of the place. She was delighted to see Jess, and even more delighted that Jess had brought a "little friend." Everyone looked round their newspapers for two small children and were disappointed to see only Jess and me.

"Now you come in the back here, little loves," boomed the enoromus lady, "and let's see what we can find for you." She led us into a staff-room place behind the bar and produced some sandwiches and buns from a carrier bag. "I was going to take them home for our Bert, but you look as if your need is greater than his." She roared laughing, disappeared for a minute and then came back carrying two orange-colored teas. "On the house, dearies. No—I insist—" as Jess began to protest. "It isn't often you come to see your Aunty Daisy nowadays, Jessie. Let me have my way this once." I wondered how on earth we could have stopped her. "I'll have to get back to my customers now, but I don't want to see any of this stuff left, mind." She looked at me sternly. "I hate waste," she concluded as she sailed majestically through the door.

Jess didn't mind me laughing. She could see I appreciated the welcome and the food, too. She told me Aunty

Daisy had known her granddad when he'd been a porter, and they were due to retire on the same day in a year's time.

"So make the most of this," she advised in Aunty Daisy's stern voice. Then she collapsed, giggling at herself. She certainly was coming out of her shell.

After we'd finished and thanked Aunty Daisy, we wandered from platform to platform looking at the people and the pigeons and glancing at each other with a huge mutual grin when a train thundered in or moved slowly out. It was bitterly cold. People huddled into their coats looking miserable and we seemed to get gayer and gayer.

Jess said, "D'you know a daft pretend game I used to play when I came here with Granddad?"

I shook my head. Her eyes were as blue as a summer sky and her hair had dried and whipped around her head in the million station drafts.

"Come on. I'll show you."

We went back to the barrier on Platform 3. People were jostling through with cases and lumpy Christmas parcels from a train that had just come in. Jess jumped up and down above them.

"The Leeds train!" she called to the ticket collector. "Which platform, please?"

He didn't even look up. "Twelve."

She rounded on me, her eyes huge. "We'll never do it! Quick—which papers do you want?" She pulled me over to the bookstall. I was completely bewildered. "Quick!" she said.

"Um. *The Times*?" I couldn't think of anything else.

"Right." She flipped down the counter to where no one

was serving and made a few gestures. Then she was back grabbing my sleeve, her nylon mack flying open. "I got a magazine for myself. Come on, else we shall miss it."

We took the steps down to the underpass three at a time and tore through the crowds weaving in and out—proper, hurrying, seasoned passengers. I began to get the feel of it.

We started up the steps to Platform 12 and Jess stopped halfway.

"I've got stitch—oh, my side—!"

"Keep going. We've got about an eighth of a minute!" I shot past her. My head was above ground level. Sure enough, a train was drawing slowly and powerfully out. The guard hung nonchalantly out of his window. He didn't even look at me as I tore along behind the tail lamp until I got right to the end of the platform.

I looked round and there was Jess skimming along toward me. "It's no good," I said. "We missed it."

We stood out there in the pouring rain, smiling huge smiles as if we'd done something great.

I said, "How did you know a train for Leeds was due?"

"I know most of the main-line trains. I get the time-table and plan trips sometimes. There's one from the bay on the other side of Platform Three in five minutes' time. That's a local to Severn Beach."

"Shall we go for it?"

She nodded and we were away, diving down the underpass and coming up the other side in a welter of people all staring at us and making way hastily. This time we caught it. The rackety diesel set was still throbbing away, with its doors standing open and its driver munching a sandwich on the step. We leaned against a platform trolley gasping and giggling.

She tried to explain. "You see, you leave it as late as you can each time. You can delay yourself by buying a magazine or going up on the wrong platform. One time the guard stopped the train for me. It was terrible."

"What did you do?"

"Pretended I was meeting someone off it."

Doors slammed and the little train for Severn Beach groaned away and we watched it regretfully. It would have been great to really catch it.

"I'll have to go now. Seriously." Jess said.

I wanted to go with her but I had my return bus ticket and no other money, so I waved her cheerio instead. She was only going twenty miles and if I went to school on Monday I should see her. I might even see her tomorrow in the village. Or this evening.

But I still felt terrible standing there waving while she got smaller and the rain and wind flipped her hair around.

9

I only just beat Mum to it that night, and as I let myself into the house the phone was ringing like mad. A repeat performance of two weeks ago.

It was Dad.

"I came out as usual at eleven-thirty and you weren't there."

"We left it that I'd—"

"I know how we left it!" He sounded right uptight. "I've been telephoning at intervals the rest of the day. Where have you been?"

"Bristol. I've just got in." I anticipated another explosion, and added piously, "I went to buy Mum's Christmas present."

"I see," he said grimly, obviously not believing me. "Does your mother know we've had a row?" At least Dad called a spade a spade.

"No . . . I don't want her to know."

"Good. That makes two of us. Now look here, Dave, we've got to agree to disagree for a while. Never mind your opinion of me—or my opinion of you, come to that. I'll pick you up next Saturday and we'll do a film and no mention of our differences. What do you say?"

I heard someone in the background.

"Are you at Mrs. Daly's place?" I asked quickly.

He hesitated. Then he said, "What if I am? Now look here, Dave—"

"I only wondered whether you'd met Bruce yet."

"As a matter of fact, yes. Last Thursday. And we got on well."

Last Thursday. And Jess said on Friday Bruce was suddenly—what had she said? Moody.

"Did you hear me, Dave? You're surprised, I suppose."

"No, not really. He's a good bloke. Did you—er—mention about me? Being your son, I mean?"

"Not yet. You didn't seem keen on him knowing, if you remember. Besides, Maggie tells me you've stopped your visits to Underwood, so there seemed little point—"

"No. Quite. Well, don't tell him, Dad. And don't let Mrs. Daly tell him either. I'd rather do it myself. In my own time."

I felt rotten. But it worked. I could feel Dad warming up.

"Okay. Does that mean you're going to start visiting him again? He'd like that, Dave. He thinks a terrific lot of you, and Maggie said—" This was getting too sickeningly intimate for my liking.

"I go again on Monday afternoon." I wanted to know why Bruce was "moody." If he felt the same way as I did about his mother and father, he would prove an invaluable ally. Besides . . . I wanted to go.

"Jolly good. That's really good, Dave. I'm pleased and Maggie will be delighted when I tell her."

"Is she listening now?"

"Of course not. Dave, you don't know Maggie. She isn't like that. Immediately she knew I was through to you, she went into another room."

"Sorry." It was like apologizing to Daly herself, and I had a job to say it.

"Okay. Easy does it, anyway. Step by step." Dad would be tapping out some Morse any minute now. "Now, how about next weekend, Dave? Any special film you'd like to see?"

"Look, Dad. I'm not being funny or anything. But there's this Buff Harkins—you remember Buff Harkins— his folks make pots and things—" Dad made a sound of assent, and I went on fast. "He wants me to have a couple of weeks with him." I left out the North Devon bit. "I haven't asked Mum yet, but if she's agreeable you wouldn't mind, would you? He's a good bloke and it will be all right with his parents and all."

There was a long pause while Dad tried to find a catch in it.

I said, "I'll get Mum to phone you, if you like."

That clinched it.

"Righto, Dave. Do that then. So I won't see you for a bit?" Did he sound relieved?

"Not till after Christmas, probably. I've got a card and I'll write you from Buff's."

"And you're happy to let things . . . simmer . . . for a while?"

"Yes."

He asked about Mum, and I crossed my fingers and said she was all right. He didn't ask about the house—course, he'd seen it for himself that morning. I sent my love to Gran and Gramps, and that was that. I'd only got Buff and Mum to worry about now. I tried to feel pleased about it, but though I couldn't have gone to Dad for Christmas I wished he'd been a bit more pressing. When I thought about it, he'd put it to me on *that* afternoon as Gran's suggestion. Not his.

The weekend was nice. I avoided lying to Mum by telling her straight off I'd spent the afternoon shopping and then exploring Temple Meads. I kept saying "we," and naturally she assumed I meant Dad. When she asked about the Christmas arrangements, I said, "It's all fixed. Don't worry about it."

80

On Monday morning we had a math test before break, and afterward I actually volunteered to clean the hard paintbrushes for next term. Then I got into the cafeteria quick and saved a place for Buff.

He came in looking a bit perkier than he had last Thursday, but not much. He was with Mart Coles and a couple of girls, and it sounded like they were going on with the euthanasia discussion. They looked around at the usual hurly-burly, and when I signaled Buff and held up one finger he grabbed his tray and came straight across.

It had been euthanasia.

"I just can't understand Mart," he said straight off through his first mouthful of chips. "He's supposed to take it easy because of his flipping heart, yet he was all for bumping off the weakest. He sounded like Hitler."

"He thinks he pulls his weight in the community because of his intellect," I said sagely, watching him oust a first-year so he and the two girls could sit at the same table. "Besides, he's only got to take it easy when it's games. He doesn't like games."

Buff sniggered. He concentrated on eating for a bit while I wondered how to lead up to the jackpot.

Then he said, "I'm glad to have a chance to talk to you, Winnie. I'm in a hell of a hole."

Here it came. Jasper was blackmailing him or something. Trust Jasper to go too far and make it impossible for me to do a thing.

"It's about Mart, actually. See, my parents know his parents. And they want me to ask Mart to go with Jem and me to Woolacombe next week."

"Next week?"

"When we break up. On the Friday. I told Mum about you and Jas and Rorie and me hitchhiking down and borrowing the cottage, and Jem said not likely, we'd wreck it. Then I kept on and on and he said he'd come with us—borrow this transit van and bring some of his stuff back. Well, that wouldn't have been too bad—"

"Great," I applauded enthusiastically.

"Then Mum says not that Jasper Ingham. And what about Martin Coles instead. And she goes and rings up his mother."

"Oh, hell," I said.

"Exactly. What a fortnight. Stuck down there with Mart Coles. Not only that, Jasper's got it in for me because he thinks I'm backing out."

"Yeah. I thought as much. I'll tell him it's not your fault."

Buff mopped his plate with his last remaining chip.

"The thing is, Winnie, I'm stuck with Mart."

"Yeah." I watched him gloomily. With his mum well in with Mart's mum I couldn't see much prospect of changing the arrangements.

"I wondered . . . I know you don't go overboard on Mart but you don't exactly hate him. I mean, if you came along it wouldn't be so bad. I know it's a lot to ask. It won't be much fun without Jas and Rorie. . . ." He tailed off because I was staring at him openmouthed. Not, as he thought, with horror, but with admiration. Okay, so it wouldn't be so much fun without Jasper, but it would be more peaceful. And so beautifully, wonderfully respectable. Even Mum couldn't object to me having a trip to

82

Devon with big-brother Jem and dear ole pal Mart Coles.

"It's terrific," I breathed. Buff looked nervous.

"Mum won't stand for Jasper," he reminded me.

"No. That's too bad. But we must learn to bear it." A thought occurred to me. "How will she feel about me horning in, though, Buff? I'm not in the Mart Coles class and she doesn't know my mum or anything."

"Oh, she likes you. She's always saying how well you take . . . well, you know. Not having your dad at home and that."

She was sorry for me. Any other time I'd have told Buff to stuff his cottage where it hurt most. But not this time.

"That's okay then," I said as smooth as butter. "Put it to her. See what she says. Any chance of her phoning my mum?"

"Sure." Buff was his usual sunny self. And I didn't feel too bad in spite of poor old Jasper. He'd hate North Devon anyway. Not a hippie in sight and just rolling moorland. Not Jasper's scene.

I just caught the one-thirty bus, and Jess was already in the sideways seat behind the driver looking prim in her school uniform.

"Hi." We grinned at one another, remembering Saturday.

The bus driver turned and watched us knowingly. He was the same one as before. Jess smiled at him, too. He was suddenly an old friend.

10

Bruce was sitting very still in the middle of the acrylic conservatory place, just his right arm lashing out now and then.

I stood in the doorway.

"Hi."

He looked up, and his broody expression changed. He tried to shove his chair toward me and only succeeded in going round in a tight circle.

"Inebriated again, I see." If he was going to be a journalist, he'd have to get used to long words. I stopped him, avoided his arms and grinned down superciliously. "If only you wouldn't mix your drinks."

He laughed, then sobered straightaway. "Gosh. Am I glad to see *you*, David." It was better than all the welcoming yells and grins I'd had from the workroom. They were all glad to see me, but Bruce was—well, almost relieved.

I checked up quickly. "Any special reason?"

He looked at me. He couldn't have lied if he'd taken lessons.

"Not really. Things have been a bit—rough."

"That's tough." I took it at its face value. Why should Bruce want to tell me about his mother's new "friend"? But he didn't like it, that was obvious. My heart leapt up again, but I had a nasty ache in the bottom of my stomach, too. If the worst came to the worst and Dad married Daly, I could put up with it—shut him right out of my life. Bruce couldn't.

He told me what had been happening the previous week, and we made up a crazy news article about it and I typed it just as inexpertly as he'd done.

Then he asked me to come to the Underwood Christmas party.

"Sure," I said before I realized Daly would be there.

"I'm longing for my mother to meet you, Dave. I keep talking about you."

"Yeah. Sure." I swallowed. "Will your father be at the party, too?"

"He's dead." He grinned in case I was embarrassed. "So he won't be."

"Oh. No." I grinned, too. I was embarrassed, but not because of Bruce's father. Quite honestly, I don't think death is such a bad thing. "When is this party, Bruce? I'll have to get time off school and it might not be easy." That could be my excuse, of course.

"Friday week. It'll go on till about six, I expect."

Friday week. The twelfth. We broke up that day, and I should be well on my way to North Devon with Jem Harkins, Buff and Mart Coles by six o'clock. Mum's operation would be over. I crossed my fingers.

"Blast. I don't know whether I can make it that day, Bruce." I thought quickly. Everything I told Bruce stood a chance of getting back to Dad. But if Buff kept his promise and his mum rang mine . . . well, it'd be all official anyway, wouldn't it? "I've got some pretty wild plans for this Christmas."

He was momentarily disappointed. Then he brightened.

85

"Tell," he commanded.

So I told him. As if I was talking to Jas. All Humphrey Bogart and hip stuff. He was convulsed. And envious. He'd never hinted at feeling—well, deprived, before, and he didn't really this time. It was just so obvious that he couldn't rough it in some cottage like we were going to do.

He made the trip sound Boy Scouty and jolly good fun, et cetera.

"I have pretend games like that," he told me. "You know, where I have to make a shelter from boughs and light a fire and sniff out water, and things like that."

"Great stuff. Did Jess tell you about her pretend game? On the railway station?"

"No."

"I'll get her." I went out to the workroom and called Jess. To be honest, I couldn't take much more on my own. I still liked Bruce, we got on. But I was beginning to feel guilty. Like Miss Ruskin had said back in November, did I owe something to Bruce? Because my body worked and his didn't?

Jess came in hung with little kids like a Christmas tree. Between us, we told them all how to play the last-minute-passenger. We did actions. Mrs. Preston came in to see what the row was about.

"There's never any fuss like this when Jessamy comes alone," she told me severely. Bruce winked at me.

The week went too fast toward December fifth. Mrs. Harkins telephoned one evening and put things right with Mum. I'd already genned her up and done some pleading, and she must have guessed how I felt about going to Gran's with the possibility of having to meet Daly, because she accepted gracefully. Then she telephoned Gran and explained about my invitation to North Devon. Dad wasn't in, of course. Gran seemed to ask a lot of questions, and Mum answered brightly. She didn't say anything about her operation.

I said, "The only thing is, you're going to be in the hospital, either at Bristol or here, and no visitors for a couple of weeks."

Mum said, "Don't you believe it, my lad. All the staff from the Home will be calling. And your aunts will come down, that's for certain." Mum's two sisters lived in London and had been a bit funny about the divorce.

"Yes, but—"

"No buts, David. I shall be very pleased you can't come to see me every blessed day. It's no place for a young boy. You enjoy this cottage place with the Harkins boys. As a matter of fact, I'm delighted you'll be away from that Jasper Ingham for a bit. I met his mother in the village the other day, and she was rather unpleasant."

I told her about my heavy-breathing act. She tried not to smile.

"Honestly, Dave. When will you grow up! Still, Buff Harkins is a good influence. And I think that Martin Coles is a lovely boy."

Most adults think that about Mart.

So I was all set. Just Mum's operation to get through.

Friday came. I told Bruce not to expect me because I was taking my mum into the hospital. It didn't bother him; he was used to hospitals. He told me some stories that cheered me up a lot—he was so matter-of-fact. Jess told me quietly there was nothing to worry about. I'd known that was what she would say.

The news got around school, too. Miss Ruskin asked if I would be coming in next week. When I said yes, she suggested I cut out the Underwood visits and use the time to visit the hospital. She was nice. No questions about how I was going to manage. She was offering what help she could, and that was that. Later she handed me the printed program of *The Mikado,* which was coming off on the Thursday. There was a list of names under "Scenery," alphabetically arranged. It took me a minute to spot "Jessamy Henshawe" and "David Winterbourne." I felt myself blushing.

"Take it to show your mother," Miss Ruskin said. "And there's a supper for cast and helpers after the show. Try to make it."

I was going to make an excuse, like I always do for any school activities, but suddenly I knew that if I didn't go neither would Jess.

"Thanks, Miss," I mumbled. I turned away; then I said over my shoulder, "I've enjoyed it. Doing the painting. And hearing about those old birds. Gilbert and Sullivan."

She didn't say anything. When I looked back from the end of the corridor, she was still standing outside the staff-room door watching me.

Then it was Friday, and Mum was giving me all the instructions she'd given me the night before and trying to act as if she was off on a cruise somewhere. It was horrible. We sat at the breakfast table and didn't eat a thing.

Mum said, "Now, my laundry. And yours, of course.

Doris will do that down at the Home. Just go in the back door—"

"Okay, Mum. I know where the laundry room is."

"Good. I've canceled the milk completely. You can buy what you want from Cooky's when you get the bread. The housekeeping money is in that brown teapot. I've put ten pounds separately in an envelope for your trip with the Harkins boys. Take your postoffice savings book in case you need more."

"Sure. Okay, Mum."

"Mind you take plenty of underpants and socks with you—"

"Sure. Don't *worry*, Mum."

"Who's worrying? I'm looking forward to the rest and I know I can trust you. There's nothing to worry about."

"Of course not."

"Just remember to switch off the electricity and water when you go."

"I might not go. I'll have to see."

"Dave! Don't be silly. I want you to go. If you don't, I shall write to Gran and—"

"Okay, okay." I looked at her cup full of cold tea. "Shall I pour that down the sink?"

She looked at it, sighed, and sort of flopped.

"Sorry, love. I'm just a little bit nervous."

I wanted to hug her. I wanted to cry. I sort of grinned. "Same here."

It wasn't quite so bad after that. I carried her case to the bus stop and it was raining and we didn't see anyone we knew. She seemed sort of dependent; she let me help her up on the bus and pay her fare. That kind of thing.

We got to the hospital, and it reminded me of Temple Meads station; people hurrying around purposefully, as if they'd got a train to catch, and others standing or sitting, anxiously waiting. Mum was going off on a journey, and I was going to be doing the waiting. She was at home like Jess had been at home in the station. I think she'd done her training here—years ago, of course, but stations and hospitals never really change. She wasn't worried anymore, not about herself. She went off with some nurse, already chatting as if she'd known her years, and when I went into the ward—it was called Sopwith Ward—she was sitting up in bed all flushed and pretty and smiling, and immediately introduced me to the people either side of her.

"This is my son, David," she told them. I thought of how it would be when she wore the bed jacket. . . . Please, God, let her wear the bed jacket and show it off to her mates. . . . Please, God, let her be all right.

"Sylvia's in for the same as me," she confided in a lower tone as I sat on a daft low chair and gazed up at her in the high bed. "But she's got three kids and her husband can't afford to take time off, so they're being fostered. We've got a lot to be thankful for, haven't we, Dave?"

I said, "Yeah. Sure. Who's Sylvia?"

Mum swiveled her eyes to the right. "I just introduced you, idiot." Her eyes switched to the left. "That side's not saying much. Perhaps she's got you-know-what."

It all sounded pretty ghoulish. I didn't like Mum entering into it all so wholeheartedly. The train was pulling out taking her away, and she was laughing instead of weeping.

90

She kicked me out soon after that, because she wanted me to be home before it was dark. It was only three o'clock. I stood outside the hospital and listened to the rain on the hood of my parka and held on to Mum's case containing her outdoor clothes as if I were hanging on to a life belt. I'm usually pretty busy at three o'clock most afternoons, and looking forward to getting the cloth on the table ready for Mum to come in at six. Now I'd got nothing to do, no deadlines to meet and no Mum. The rain sounded different; it even smelled different. I tried to think of Jasper, of Buff and the trip to North Devon, and they seemed unreal. I remembered Jasper's sneer as he called me "Mummy's boy." But he'd been right all the time.

I toyed with the idea of going to Broadmead and looking round the Christmas decorations. Then I remembered that Jess would be at Underwood and Bruce wouldn't be expecting me, so his face would light up and he'd flail those crazy arms of his with pleasure at the sight of my ugly mug.

I turned and walked toward the Heights.

Saturday and Sunday weren't quite so awful, because I seemed to be all day getting into and out of Bristol to see Mum. She seemed better already. Maybe she hadn't been joking when she said she needed the rest. Anyway, both times I went in, there she was sitting up all smart and perky with loads of flowers from the staff and patients at the old folks' place and the life histories of everyone around her.

"That's the thing about hospitals, Dave," she told me.

"You get so interested in everyone else, you forget about yourself. Honestly, love, I wish you could hear some of them talk. It would make you realize—we're so *lucky*!"

I tried to hang on to her voice as I walked back to the bus station. The church bells were going like mad for Evensong and the rain was sleety enough to pretend it was snow. And Mum's operation was booked for tomorrow morning.

They said she was comfortable but they wouldn't let me see her. "She's not very pretty," said a smiling Jamaican nurse. "Tubes and things."

Tuesday I was allowed to sit by her bed for exactly three minutes. She was asleep and she looked terrible. Wednesday she was sitting up, but her head was lolling back against the support thing. She smiled at me and took my hand but she didn't say much. Just for something to say myself, I started telling her about Bruce. Suddenly tears ran down her face.

"Does it hurt—shall I get the nurse?" I said urgently, leaning over her.

She shook her head wearily. "I'm fine. I just love you."

The Jamaican nurse came up then and said we were upsetting each other, which was a typical reaction on the third post-op day. I walked back to the bus station still crying into the hood of my parka and understanding why Mum had said we were so lucky.

Then Thursday she was okay. She was pale and didn't say much, but it was Mum lying there again. She'd been up, too, only to go to the bathroom, but she'd walked it on her own, and she kept asking me questions—what had

92

I had for tea yesterday and the day before and did I change into dry clothes after the paper round. Things like that. I grinned all the way home on the bus, and lots of people grinned back.

Anyway, after the dear old paper round and sausages and instant spud for tea, I got ready and went to *The Mikado*. I didn't quite have the nerve to sit by Jess, but I sat in the row behind her next to Buff and leaned forward to ask her about the supper.

"Are you going?" she asked.

"Only if you do."

"Okay."

A few weeks ago, Jess and me barely spoke. Funny how things happen. I never thought of her spots now, or her red face, or her spelling. I thought of her talking to Liz, practicing floor work, running for a train. She made me feel terrific—and very safe at the same time.

The performance was great. Every time one of our hats bobbed on and off and we at last saw the willow-pattern set as a whole—well, you know the feeling. I only just restrained myself from poking Buff and saying "I did that" like some little first-year show-off.

Miss Ruskin was unrecognizable as one of the little maids from school; she was billed on the program as Jacqueline Ruskin and I remembered how those sixth-years had called her Jackie. The one she had called Jock was Nanki-Poo. I had to admit he was good.

In the interval, the dinner ladies served pop and crisps and Buff and me had a talk about our trip.

"I'd made up my mind not to come—Mum in hospital and all. But she was so much better today . . ." I blew a reflective raspberry through my straw. "I don't know what to say, Buff. I'm dead keen to get away."

"I hope you can come, Winnie. But don't feel you've got to." Buff was good like that. "Tell you what, if you're going into Bristol tomorrow shall we pick you up outside the hospital? Then if things aren't too good . . . well, no hard feelings, eh?"

"Thanks, Buff. I'm almost certain to come."

I told Jess all about it at the supper, and she agreed that if Mum was okay there was no reason why I shouldn't go.

"She'll be transferred back here to the cottage hospital, won't she? I can go in and see her, if you like."

"Gosh. Thanks, Jess." I had a couple of good friends in Buff and Jess. Like Mum said, I was lucky.

"One thing, David." Jess was frowning and staring at the sandwich in her hand as if it was moldy or something. "You can't make the Underwood party, I suppose? Just for ten minutes?"

I pulled a face. "Not really. Buff's meeting me outside the hospital after visiting hours."

"Oh, well." She bit into the sandwich. "It's only Bruce. Since last Friday when you arrived unexpectedly, he's just gone back to how he was. You know, I told you. All quiet and not trying to do anything."

"Oh, Lord." I wished I could tell Jess the whole story. But she might think that my Underwood visits were all wrong—like Dad had. I couldn't stand it if Jess looked at me like Dad did that Saturday morning we had our row.

Then Miss Ruskin came up and asked us what we thought of Gilbert and Sullivan now, and we had quite a

94

chat, which made old Nanki-Poo look a bit down-in-the-mouth.

I wasn't going to mention the last thing that happened that Thursday. But perhaps I'd better not leave anything out. It didn't worry me a lot at the time. I was pretty good and happy that night. Mum was going to be okay and I was clearing off from all thoughts of Dad and Daly to North Devon; Jess and me had had a good evening— we were getting to be part of the in crowd that night— yes, on the whole I felt good. So when I went into the bike sheds for my bike and found Jasper and Rorie waiting for me, as I say I wasn't too bothered.

It wasn't the first time we'd fought, of course, but it was the first time I'd been in a hurry to get it over. Jess was waiting for me in the drive.

It was no holds barred. Jasper was mad; he bit into my hand when I tried to hold him off and tore a couple of buttons off my blazer. Rorie sort of galloped around getting in a kick now and then like an excited dog, but Jasper really wanted to get me.

I shoved him away and he fell over a bike; then I turned and hit Rorie hard. He went off a few yards, whimpering, and stayed there while Jasper charged in again. We wrestled and stumbled around the racks, knocking ourselves against the support posts of the shed.

I panted, "What the hell's up with you, Jas?" and he swore back and called me some names I can't write down. I gathered he thought I was some kind of traitor for not fixing him and Rorie into tomorrow's trip. I had felt a bit of a heel once or twice about it, so I let him get me one in the mouth. Then I grabbed his arm, swung him round in a wide circle and let go. He hurdled several bikes and landed up near Rorie. I could hear them carrying on like a couple of old women.

I got my bike and joined Jess.

Perhaps it was her almighty concern about my bleeding mouth that made me feel good, or perhaps the general goodness of the day wasn't even damaged.

Anyway, I walked her to her gate; then I cycled home. I found I was singing "Once in Royal David's City."

You often get a good day like that just before everything goes wrong, don't you?

11

Friday. I packed my rucksack, rolled my sleeping bag in plastic, switched off electricity, gas and water, went to school.

Normally last day of term we wouldn't do a thing, but this time I found myself put in charge of ten first-years and told to keep them out of everyone's hair till eleven-thirty, which just shows they thought I was "worthy of responsibility," as our Head puts it. I took them up on the common. We played chain-touch till we were sweating, then collected fir cones for Christmas decorations. It wasn't too bad.

Jasper and Rorie weren't at school. Mart Coles was

friendly and said, "See you later" as if he was looking forward to it. In the cafeteria, Eccles—the Games bloke—came over and said there were a couple of footballs with a bit of life left in them I could have if I wanted. I said, "Merry Christmas to you, too, sir," and he laughed his hearty-type laugh. Then I said cheerio all round and went for the bus.

Jess had a dress on underneath her mack—I was glad she had some clothes besides her uniform. She'd got a charm bracelet for Liz and I gave her one of the footballs for Bruce, which sounds crazy but they had basketball at Underwood. We chatted easily until her stop. She was still anxious about my fight with Jasper, so we didn't talk much about Bruce's possible troubles. Maybe his mother had told him she was going to marry Dad. In which case there was nothing I could do about anything. It was just as well I was dropping out of things for a bit.

Jess hoped I'd have a nice time and a good Christmas, and she promised to go and see Mum; then she got off at Church Road and stood waving till the bus went round the next corner.

Mum was fine, really fine. I reckon she and the Sylvia woman in the next bed were having a kind of race as to who could get better quickest. Mum was winning. I told her about Jess coming to see her, and she was very pleased.

"Next time I see you, it'll be after Christmas," I said, feeling a bit hollow all of a sudden. "Are you sure—"

"We've been through this before, Dave," Mum said firmly. "I want you to get away for a bit. You could do with a change."

I made some crack about her taking it easy in her four-star hotel, and she said, "Don't make me laugh, Dave, it hurts." Then who should roll in but her two sisters from London.

She knows how I feel about them, so when she suggested I leave them to their "woman talk" I gave her a grateful wink and left. Perhaps it was better not to have to say a proper good-bye.

But it was only quarter to three and Jem Harkins wasn't picking me up till quarter past four. I didn't want to break into my money drinking tea in a cafe somewhere, so I started to walk. After ten minutes, I found myself at the bottom of Church Road. I humped my rucksack further up my back and started up toward Underwood.

Now, the next bit's important. No one was expecting me at Underwood; I hadn't even mentioned it to Mum. . . . Jess would say it was Fate and in a way it was, except that that sounds as if I'm making an excuse for what happened. And I'm not.

Anyway, for once it wasn't raining and there was a bit of a sun and I was in that mood where I could have jumped for the Box Kite in the city museum and swung across from gallery to gallery like Tarzan. So when I looked up the hill and saw Bruce bowling toward me in his wheelchair—not even a coat over his jeans and sweater—I didn't panic. I felt I could cope. . . . I could mold events. Master of the situation and all that crap.

I jumped in front of him and just stopped him before he careened off the curb. We sort of galloped on together for a few yards; then I managed to push the brake forward.

I started to yell, "What the hell d'you think you're

98

playing at?" and at the same time he was yelling at me to get round the corner, and then we both shut up and glared at each other, panting our heads off.

"You're running away," I said at last, and for the first time his arms jerked and then were still.

He tried to take a leaf out of my book. "So what?" he said, all tough and hard. "It's a free country, isn't it?"

I said, "What gave you that idea?" I stared at him some more. His face wasn't white; it was putty-colored and there was dried ice cream round his mouth. "Didn't you like the party or something?"

"No. It was rotten." He twisted convulsively and looked toward the Heights. "Look, Dave. Just get me round the corner out of sight, will you?"

There was something about him. Something that reminded me of the time I'd left Dad chatting with Daly and ran for the bus. Just for now, Bruce Daly had to get away. So I wheeled him round the corner double quick and without any more chatting, and just along past two shuttered shop fronts there was a derelict graveyard. I lugged the chair up three steps—it was hard work and my rucksack wasn't helping—and shoved and yanked him behind a boxlike tomb.

"Okay?" I asked, holding my side and breathing deeply.

He looked grateful for a minute, then terribly sad. "Okay, Dave. Thanks."

We didn't say anything for about ten minutes then. I was feeling excited—not nervous—and he just sat slumped to one side, apparently reading the inscription on the tomb thing and occasionally waving his arms back elbows first. At last he sat up straight; whether he thought they'd

99

had time to get down Church Road and look for him I've no idea, but he seemed to think some crisis was past.

"Were you coming to the party after all, Dave?" he asked.

I nodded. "I had over an hour to kill between coming out from the hospital and meeting Buff. So I thought I'd have a look at you all."

"You came up last Friday unexpectedly, too. As if you were coming to see a friend."

"Well, I was, wasn't I, nit? You're my friend, aren't you?"

"I want to be. I've always wondered, though, if you were just sorry for me."

I looked at him sharply, then away. He was a smart one.

"That's below the belt, kiddo." I hesitated. "I came up last Friday 'cause I wanted something. And I got it."

"What was that?"

"Comfort, that's what. I was right down—didn't know who to turn to . . . all that crap. I turned to you. Okay?"

He gave a half smile. "Yeah. I'm glad. Makes it all right for me to turn to you, doesn't it?"

"Sure, Bruce." I felt like a king. "Spill the beans."

He put his hand on his head, then straight up in the air. With great concentration he brought it down again and scratched his head.

"You were right. I am running away. Not just from the party."

"Yikes," I murmured. I wanted to ask how someone in a wheelchair runs away, but of course I didn't.

"There's a reason why, Dave. A good reason. D'you believe that?"

100

"Yes," I said without any hesitation at all. I wondered if now was the time to tell him why I believed him, why I understood exactly how he was feeling.

"Then help me. Take me with you to Devon—you can pretend you found me—I've lost my memory except I know I live in Devon. Maybe there's a home down there will take me in. Please, Dave—you've got to—I can't go back."

It all came in a flood like that. Like the first-year gabbles this morning. After all, he wasn't very old.

I said slowly, "It's as bad as that, is it?"

He took another breath. "You told me how easygoing the Harkinses are. They won't start making a lot of inquiries—no one will know where we've gone—no one will know I'm *with* you even—"

"Hang on, Bruce." His eyes were really wild and his arms were going like crazy. "What about your mother?"

"It's because of her. I can't explain now. You wouldn't understand."

"I understand. But . . . I mean, sorry to bring this up, kid, but how will you manage without her?"

"That's what they teach us at school. How to manage. I can go to the lavatory, wash. Things like that. I won't make you look a fool, Dave."

"Christ. I wasn't thinking of that. It's you. If you're ill or something. I mean, you take tablets—"

"I've got them. I always carry them on me. Dave, you will take me with you, won't you?"

As I said before, it's no good blaming Fate. I felt able to manage my own affairs just then. And Bruce's, too, if I had to. But to be fair to myself, there was something about Bruce just then. Something wild and unpre-

101

dictable. One way or another, he meant to escape.

I said foolishly, "I can't leave you here, can I?"

He relaxed quite suddenly, sagging down into his chair like a sack of spuds. His arms hung limply over the chrome wheels. He grinned sheepishly.

I began thinking aloud. "Not to Devon, though." Strange I'd never really believed in Devon. Bruce didn't protest; he was willing to leave everything to me now. I thought of the long three-hour drive through the winter-dark countryside with Mart Coles and Buff and felt a sharp pang of regret; then I stopped thinking of all that. Positive thinking was what I needed now. . . . When had I said that to myself before? I went on speaking softly, "We mustn't let anyone else in on this. No one else would understand." Except maybe Jess, and I didn't want to involve Jess in what I already knew would be trouble. "But we don't want to make Buff and Company suspicious. So . . . we go back to the hospital and tell them I can't leave Mum." Of course. It was so simple. They wouldn't be surprised. "Then we go back to my place. It's empty. If we live in the back and don't show any lights, nobody will know we're there. We can lie low till Christmas, anyway."

"We'll think of something else then," Bruce said with a trusting confidence that was somehow unnerving.

"Sure," I said largely. Perhaps two weeks without Bruce would be enough to convince Mrs. Daly that her marriage plans were ill-advised. I liked that phrase. Ill-advised. It made what we were doing somehow judicious.

I went over it all carefully. Dad wouldn't connect Bruce's disappearance with me, because I was in Devon,

102

and even if Buff telephoned his parents and mentioned I wasn't with them, they would naturally assume I was staying at Gran's. In fact, I would tell Buff that was where I was going. So that I could be near Mum.

Bruce said, "Let's get going then."

"Not you. You stay here. It's okay; I'm not going to leave you, I'll be back. Look, here's my watch. It's ten to four, okay? I should be back by half past. It'll be dark by then and we shan't be so conspicuous." He started to protest. "Don't be daft, Bruce. They're sure to be out looking for you—we'd be spotted a mile off."

"Leave your rucksack then."

"You don't trust me!"

"It's not that. It's creepy in here with all these old graves."

"I was going to leave it anyway, nit."

I sorted through the pockets and came up with some chewing gum and an old book of Dad's on woodcraft I'd slipped in for a laugh. Bruce had always seemed practically my own age in the security of Underwood. He looked small now. And cold. I unstrapped my sleeping bag and tucked it round him inexpertly.

Then I left him.

It was queer walking back into the city. I was still exhilarated—more than before, probably. I'd imagined I was dropping out of the problem of Dad and Daly, that there was nothing else I could do about it. Now I was right in the middle of it. I was like a puppet master and they were the puppets. And what a change that was!

It had gone very cold, and there were a lot of people around. Tons of students from the University—all wearing duffels, so if Bartlett was out looking for Bruce he'd never recognize me.

I got to the hospital at ten past four, and Jem was already parked in the visitors' car park.

I went over and made a regretful face as I started in on my story.

They weren't surprised, of course, but it hurt when Buff was so disappointed. Even Jem said, "Look, shall we come and see your mother? You're sure you're not overanxious?"

Buff said, "Jem could have a word with the Sister or something."

"No. Honestly. I couldn't come. I'd be a ruddy nuisance always wanting to phone up. I'm going up to stay with my gran for a few days. I'm really sorry to let you down."

They had to accept it. It would be better for them in a way. I'd have split Mart and Buff good and proper. Without me, they'd get on quite well. Still, it was funny waving them good-bye. And funnier still walking back to that old churchyard in the twilight. I really was on my own now.

Bruce was pathetically glad to see me. I suppose it was rotten sitting there helplessly, always in the power of other people.

"We'll sit it out till it's completely dark," I told him. "Then we'll make tracks."

"How far is it, Dave?"

"Fifteen miles, I suppose. Yes, about that."

I was rummaging in my sack again for the hunky sandwiches I'd cut that morning.

"Fifteen miles?" Bruce sounded scared. "How are we going to get there?"

I looked at him, surprised. Of course, minibus to school and back, and Daly probably had a car. He just wasn't used to walking. Or, rather, being walked.

I said impatiently, "Shanks' pony, of course. How do you think?"

"You'll never make it, Dave. These chairs are awkward."

I remembered the difficulty of lugging it up the churchyard steps, but I grinned.

"We've got all night. And you can carry the rucksack."

We sat quietly and munched a cheese sandwich. We were thirsty—I'd been going to buy a drink on the way. But there was nothing to be done about it then.

At five o'clock, we left the comparative safety of the old tombs. Gingerly I maneuvered the chair down the steps and walked as far away from the streetlights as I could. If only it had been five weeks earlier, Bruce would have passed as a Guy Fawkes, what between the rucksack and the sleeping bag. As it was, I hoped we looked like a moonlight flit.

It was going to be a long night.

12

Jasper reckoned he'd had to walk home once after going into Bristol for a late-night horror film. He said it took him four hours, which I suppose is about right if he didn't stop for a rest or anything. It took Bruce and me eight hours and fifteen minutes. I honestly don't know how we did it.

At first it was still exciting. Like something on telly. I had no doubts about what we were doing—it all seemed so inevitable. All I had to worry about was outwitting whoever might be searching for us. It would be the police by now, of course.

So I got us off the road as soon as I could. Instead of going across the Cumberland Basin, I went through the park underneath it, which meant using that old swing bridge across the Avon. They only use that when the big bridge is open for shipping to go through. It was completely deserted when we got there, rush hour and all. But it was nasty in the park. Empty enough for us to stick out like a couple of sore thumbs.

After a few people looked at us curiously, I got off the path and right away from the lights. Only trouble was, the grass was muddy and Bruce's chair had those small front wheels, which sank right up to the hubs straightaway. In the end I had to turn the chair backward, tip him up and lug him across at an angle.

Bruce spotted the patrol car at the Long Ashton junction.

"It's okay," I whispered. "There's always a police car there to check any speedo's."

"What are we going to do?"

He sounded panicky; he hadn't liked the jolting ride across the park and he hadn't got the feeling of adventure I had. I couldn't believe we weren't going to win. Things had worked out too well for failure. Bruce was desperate—but then maybe he had never wanted to jump for the Box Kite in the museum.

I laughed. "Go back a bit. Get across the traffic and up past Ashton Park."

"It's too quiet."

"Not tonight, sweetheart. City are playing Sunderland at home. The lane between the ground and that pub will be packed with supporters."

We couldn't go wrong. Kickoff was at seven and we hit the supporters' route at just the right time. You hear a lot about football crowds, but when this lot saw Bruce in the chair they couldn't have been nicer.

"Going to the match, lad?"

"Here. Have my hat—" Bruce managed a grin as a red-and-white beret was crammed on his head.

"Come up the East End, boyo—you'll bring us luck!"

They brought us luck. We were past the Park Lodge and grunting and panting up the long coombe to the old Roman ridge road. We were out of Bristol. And no one had stopped us.

Then it got tough. The excitement sort of oozed out of my old desert boots—I wasn't frightened of being caught anymore. There were wide verges either side of the road shoulder high with ferns; when I heard a car coming, I shoved Bruce into them and stood with my back to the road as if I was having a pee. The real danger had gone and the slog had started.

By the time we got to the top of the ridge, it was eight o'clock and I reckoned we'd done four miles. Three hours to walk four miles! At that rate, we wouldn't be home before it was light. Still, I had to stop for a rest and a sandwich.

The sleeping bag round Bruce was soaked from the

107

wet ferns. I took it off and gave it a good shake. It only took about a minute, but when I tucked him back up he was shivering convulsively. I was sweating.

"Hell—" I pinioned his arms to his knees—yes, even his knees were jumping as he shivered. "You can't be that cold. Get that hand down under your bum—go on, sit on it." We struggled like a couple of wrestlers.

"It's okay. I don't mind. Honestly."

The moon came out from a cloud and I got a good look at him. Had he been as thin-faced as this sitting in front of his typewriter in that conservatory place? His nose was running and he was dribbling. I pulled out my hanky and wiped his face without any gentleness.

"I'm sorry, Dave," he said.

"Shut up. It's all right." I jammed and wedged the sleeping bag around him, then set my kit bag on his lap to stop him flailing it loose. For the first time, I felt a worm of fear wriggle in my stomach. Bruce was not like other boys. While he was sitting still in that chair, his circulation was bound to slow right down. I noticed my breath billowing out in a cloud of vapor; his was a wispy mist.

"For God's sake, breathe properly," I snapped. "Come on. Do it with me. In . . . two, three, four—no, don't let it go yet, you fool. I said *four!* Try it again. In . . . two, three, four. Now blow it out! Make a cloud. Can't you do better than that? Do it again—try and beat me."

We sat up there, looking down on the lights of Bristol, sucking and blowing as if our lives depended on it. Maybe Bruce's did. I got my hand under the sleeping bag and felt his ankle. It was stone cold. But then he couldn't feel his

108

legs anyway, so maybe they were always cold. I didn't know. The number of things I didn't know about Bruce began to pile up.

I said tentatively, "Look. Kiddo. You going to be all right? We could stop the next car—call it all off—"

"No!" Somehow he jerked his arm free and the elbow caught on the chair back with a resounding crack. He ignored it. "Dave, *please*. You promised. We can't turn back now—we've got over the worst bit! I told you— I can't go back!" He blew an enormous vapor cloud. "Look—I'm all right—" He blew again. A failure. We both laughed.

"Okay. We'd better get on then. Get that arm inside."

I tried to walk solidly for another hour, but I couldn't quite make it. By nine o'clock, I was shoving the chair at arms' length, with my body at an angle leaning on it and my head right down between my hands. We kept scuffing into the grass verge or veering across the road when the lights of a car started flickering in the trees. I gave up hiding Bruce and just trudged on regardless. No one stopped. You can get away with anything in this country.

We rested and went on. I made Bruce talk for a bit, thinking it would be bad for him to fall asleep. Then he slumped further and further to one side and the small wispy cloud still hovered in front of his mouth, so I let him stay.

At eleven o'clock, we passed one of those asbestos bungalows people used to be able to stick up without planning permission. A light shone through an uncurtained window and showed a kitchen and an old bloke pouring boiling water into a teapot.

109

I was dying of thirst. And I was terrified about Bruce. I jammed the chair behind a couple of rhododendrons by the gate and knocked on the door. The old man was a cautious one.

"Who is it?" he yelled from the other side.

"I've missed the bus, sir," I said in my best voice, trying to cut out the bass bit and shove up the falsetto. "I wondered if I could have a drink. It's a chilly night."

That was a laugh. A chilly night forsooth.

A little transom suddenly opened up above me, and the old chap's head came out. My God, he *was* cautious. He must be standing on some steps or something.

"On your own, are you? I'm not on the phone."

"It's all right, sir. I don't want the phone. I told my family what happened. I don't mind walking."

I tried to sound like Mart Coles. Responsible. It seemed to work.

"It's certainly a cold night." The old chap peered from left to right. "I've just made a pot of tea."

I decided to be frank and guileless. "I saw you, sir. That's what made me knock. But not if it's any trouble."

I was in. Not through the front, though. That was locked for the winter and there *was* a pair of steps leaning against it. I went in through the back, and it was immediately locked after me. A long passage led to the front and there were rooms off to right and left. We went into the kitchen.

"Nice little place you have here, sir." I don't know how I managed this sort of talk. I could barely stand still for thinking of Bruce out there alone and freezing.

"Built it myself. Nineteen twenty-four." He poured out

110

two mugs of tea and heaped sugar into them. "Right out in the wilds I was then. Even now in the winter I have a job getting supplies. Where you from, lad?"

I lied. "Wraxall. Not far now."

"Teach you to be sure of the last bus, though, eh?"

I laughed ruefully as I took the tea. I warmed my hands against the mug and took a steaming sip. The old chap went on and on. How he'd built the bungalow and badgered the electric company for "juice." How his wife had died in the war and he'd buried their wedding ring underneath the weeping willow in the back garden. How their daughter found it too much trouble to come and see him and he'd given up the pub because the landlord watered the beer. He was so glad to see someone who would listen he'd have given me a bed.

I managed to top up the mug without him noticing; then I went over to the sink and turned on the tap, pretending to rinse it.

"That was smashing, sir." I held the mug straight down so the steam would go up my sleeve. "Thanks a million."

"Call again, son. I'd be pleased to see you any time. It's nice to have a little chat."

I hated stealing that mug. He would have given it me, I know. Funny how many lonely people there are and how easy it is to deceive them. And how hateful. But that tea did wonders for Bruce.

I lugged him out of the rhododendrons handle-first and got him a few yards down the road; then I shook him.

"Come on, Bruce. Wakey, wakey. Nice hot cuppa . . ."

I had a hell of a job to bring him to. Even when he was

111

drinking, he didn't seem to remember where he was or
what had happened. I ferreted around for the last sandwich and soaked a corner of it in the tea and pushed it
into his mouth. Then I scraped the syrupy sugar from the
bottom of the mug onto a crust and told him to suck it.
After a bit, he seemed to revive and managed a feeble
grin.

"Not much farther, kiddo," I said heartily, rubbing my
hands over the sleeping bag in a crazy effort to get his
circulation going. "You'll be in a nice warm bed by mid-
night."

"Dave . . ." He seemed to have difficulty in speaking.
"Dave . . . so good to me . . . like a brother."

I stopped massaging the sleeping bag and stayed still
for a moment crouched in front of him. His words seemed
to echo in the bare elms that lined that old road. I stared
at him, not seeing him in the darkness. Then I stood up
slowly and tilted my chin toward the cloudy night sky.
"Like a brother . . ." That's what I was fighting against,
wasn't it? And so was Bruce—though he didn't know it.
Yes, if Dad married Daly, Bruce and I would be brothers.

I frowned at the moon as it made one of its brief ap-
pearances. What the hell was I doing here? What the hell
was it all about?

There was a sound from Bruce, and I looked down
again and saw that his eyes were closing against the
moon. There was no time for worrying about the rights
and wrongs of anything then; I had to get Bruce into bed.
So I shelved the whole thing, dropped the mug into the
top of the rucksack and bent to that cursed chair again.

At quarter to one, I passed the sign about careful driv-

112

ers being welcome. I'd intended going back ways through the town, but I wasn't caring anymore. I just kept straight on down the long main street that eventually leads to the sea, and turned off where it says "Industrial Estate." There was the gate . . . the narrow side path to the shed where my bike was . . . back-door key in my pocket; I couldn't get it into the lock. Then the door was open and I was fighting the chair to pull it into the kitchen . . . putting on the light. If anyone had seen us, or saw the light shining down the back garden now, that was it.

For one terrible second I thought Bruce was dead then. His head looked as if it was falling off the shapeless tube of the sleeping bag, his mouth was open and his eyes not properly shut. I grabbed the mirror off the window ledge and held it shakingly in front of the white face. It misted.

The next half an hour was hectic. I got a second wind from somewhere and plunged around the house switching on heat wherever I could, especially in Mum's room where I intended putting him. The electric blanket, wall fire, convector heater on landing—they all went on. I raided the cocoa tin where Mum keeps the meter money and fed half a dozen tenpences into the meter. I warmed some milk from the defrosted fridge—of course it was still all right this weather—and tried to spoon it onto Bruce's mouth. But it just ran out again, so I gave that up. Then I unwrapped him and picked him up. He was so light. It was terrible how light he was. Under ninety pounds, I'd say. I'd humped some of the first-years around this morning—was it only this morning? They were much heavier than Bruce. I got him upstairs easily and dumped him in Mum's bed, jeans, sweater and all. I took off his

113

shoes and tried to rub his feet underneath the bedclothes.

It was three o'clock when he opened his eyes. The blanket was burning hot by then, but I didn't switch it down. I was frightened he'd wet it and we'd all go up in smoke but I left it on anyway, and the first word he said when he looked at me was "Lavatory."

"Okay, Bruce."

I lifted him up again and carried him to the bathroom. He wouldn't let me stay. I don't know how he managed. I leaned against the outside of the door and felt tears running into my mouth. When he called me, he was sitting on the stool washing his hands. He was still pale but he grinned at me.

"We made it, Dave."

"Yes. We made it. I was beginning to think we wouldn't."

I didn't try to hide the tears. He knew what I meant.

I tucked him up again and turned down the control knob on Mum's blanket. Then I went next door into my own room. And I slept.

13

I woke up the next day to the sound of terrific knocking at the front door. Before it had stopped, I had checked my watch and seen it was two o'clock, registered that the house was warmer than it had been for years and slid out of bed and into Mum's room.

Bruce was sitting on the edge of the bed looking almost normal. His right arm was shooting out spasmodically and hitting the wall. I ran across and pushed it down and made signals to keep quiet. Then I crept across to the net curtains and peered down.

My heart sank. Dad was standing at the front door, looking up right into my eyes. I had shrugged and was actually moving to twitch the curtain aside when his gaze swept on to the other window and I realized he couldn't see me.

I signaled to Bruce again and whipped out of Mum's room and hung over the banisters. How had I left things downstairs? Because Dad would certainly come round to the back. The bolts were on the front door, which meant I couldn't possibly have bolted the back as well. So if he had a key it was all up.

I went halfway down the stairs just as Dad fitted his key into the front door and pushed against the bolts. My heart was jumping about all over my body. Bad luck, Dad.

I peered down the hall. No light on in the kitchen and the curtains were drawn, so he couldn't see Bruce's chair. I heard him go down the side path.

I began rehearsing a speech.

"What you doing here, Dad? . . . No, I didn't go to Devon after all. Mum didn't want you to know, but she's in the hospital . . . nothing serious, really . . ."

If I could get the chair into the front room in time, I just might be able to fob him off. I got to the kitchen just as his steps reached the door. The chair was too big to ease round the cooker—it was stuck in the doorway. Dad rattled the doorknob.

"You there, Dave? Open up!"

How the hell did he know? That bloke on the old Bristol road—had he reported the loss of his flaming coffee mug?

A voice—old Rosey Firbright from next door—spoke up.

"Did you want something, Mr. Winterbourne? I'm afraid young David's gone away with a school friend for a few days."

A pause. Dad hated the Firbrights.

"I thought he might have changed his mind. It's nothing important. I'll go along to the Home and see his mother."

This was meat and drink to Ma Firbright. "Didn't you know?" she gloated. "Mrs. Winterbourne's been in hospital this past week and more. In Bristol."

Another pause. I could almost hear Dad swallowing. "No, I didn't know."

"You'd better come in and I'll tell you what I know. It's no good you trying to get in the back. Mrs. Winterbourne had the lock changed some time back when young David lost the key."

Of course she did. Good old Mum. Good, cautious old Mum.

Dad made some unwilling noises, but after a bit he moved off. There was no standing against Ma Firbright. As luck would have it, she had missed me last night, and as almost nothing ever got by her eagle eye, she would swear to anyone that I couldn't be there. It was the best bit of luck we'd had so far.

Very gently I pulled the wheelchair into the parlor

116

and covered it over with Mum's best plush tablecloth. Then I legged it back upstairs.

Bruce was sitting very still, evidently concentrating all his will on keeping his arms by his sides. I whispered the news to him gleefully and took my stand by the window to see Dad off. For the first time, I noticed Dad's old Morris parked a little way up the road. Out of sight of the downstairs windows. So he *was* suspicious. Though he was right, it hurt that he had such a lousy opinion of me.

Then I spotted Daly. She was out of the car, pacing up and down its length. I suppose Dad had told her to keep out of the way. She was wearing a sheepskin coat thing and her brown trousers, and her hair was spilling all over her shoulders. As if she couldn't be bothered to put it up.

I glanced back at Bruce, wondering whether to tell him. He was looking a bit down-in-the-mouth, just staring at the carpet. I thought I'd better shut up about his mother. He wasn't very old and he might not be able to keep from yelling to her.

Then Dad came out of next door and walked up the road. He didn't even glance back at the house this time. He took Daly's arm and they stood for a moment. Then quite suddenly she put her face down in her hands. It was awful. I turned away quickly.

"Well. That's that, kiddo. We fooled 'em," I said in a cocky American accent. It didn't come off. I looked down the street again and saw Dad tucking Daly into the front seat of the car. I could be there, going to Gran's for Christmas. Or I could be somewhere near

Woolacombe with Buff and Mart.

I sat down by Bruce. "How you feeling?" I asked soberly.

He nodded vigorously. I realized he was near tears.

"You frightened me to death last night. Are you warm now?"

He nodded again.

"Well—" I got up and rubbed my hands briskly. "Better see about breakfast or tea or whatever it is. We'll have to stay up here. It . . . it might get a bit boring. We could play cards."

"Okay," Bruce said huskily.

It was hell trying to get toast and tea quietly. Our grill pan must be the rattliest in the world and even the tea caddy made a noise like a fire alarm. I kept peering through the closed curtains to check if Firbright was in her garden, and by the time I crept back upstairs with the tray I was sweating blood.

Bruce was still quiet. He was more upset about his mum getting married again than I was about Dad. . . . No wonder, I suppose. He was so dependent on her; they must be close.

Surely Dad would realize pretty soon that he and Daly were . . . well, impossible? He'd upset me—not that that had bothered him. But now he'd practically driven Bruce away.

I wondered how long it would take.

"Don't you like tea?" I said, more to break the silence than anything.

"It's okay. I can't take it. I'll have plain milk."

"Milk?" I shoved the bottle toward him. "Go on, drink it up. It'll do you good anyway. I'll eat your toast."

118

Only after he'd polished off the milk did I realize it was our last. And of course the milkman wouldn't be calling for two weeks.

"D'you drink a lot of milk, Bruce?" I asked casually.

He nodded. "I can't digest much solid food."

"You did all right on tea and cheese sandwiches last night."

"I don't remember." He flopped listlessly back on the bed.

"Look." I felt baffled by his attitude. "There's tins of soup downstairs. Tomato. And chicken. Would you like one?"

"No." He looked at me across the tray. "Don't worry, Dave. I'm never hungry."

"Where's those tablets of yours?" I said suspiciously. "Oughtn't you to have one now?"

"I haven't got them."

"Yes, you have. You told me yesterday."

"I was lying. Don't look like that. I had to get away somehow, and you wouldn't have taken me if—"

"I thought we were friends!"

"We are. But—"

"Friends trust each other."

"I'm sorry, Dave." He didn't look all that interested in convincing me. He just looked tired.

I remembered all that I hadn't told Bruce, so I shut up and munched through the rest of the toast angrily. He just lay there staring at the ceiling.

At last I got up. "Bruce. Are you all right? Are you ill? Tell me the truth now—it's really important."

He said, "Dave. Tell *me* something. . . ." His voice was very quiet. I stooped over him. "Do you think people

119

should be kept alive when they're no use to anyone?"

I jerked upright. We were back to euthanasia again.

"Shut up talking like that," I told him roughly. "I'm not going to listen. I'll go and get the cards and a tin of soup and you're going to drink it whether you want to or not."

I slammed out of the room, forgetting about the need for silence. I cut myself opening the soup, and spilled some of it on the kitchen floor. It occurred to me I couldn't let any water down the drains in case Firbright saw it. Damn. I mopped up savagely. What was I doing, hiding out in my own house, trembling because a spastic boy seemed to have lost the will to live?

The rest of the day passed drearily. Bruce had about two spoonsful of chicken soup and retched on the third. I forced him to sit up and look at a hand of cards I dealt him behind a screen of books—he couldn't hold them. But it was hopeless. We were supposed to be playing rummy and I had to keep peering round the books at his cards to suggest things. It got dark and we could only have Mum's reading light on, and after he'd gone to the bathroom again he seemed exhausted. So I tucked him up and went downstairs for a bit.

I didn't know what to do. The escape scheme, which had seemed so terrific last night, now seemed utterly pointless. I couldn't think why I hated the idea of Dad marrying Bruce's mum anymore. It would mean I would have some kind of legal right to look after Bruce. And Mum would love him. And anyway it was because of Mum I'd hated Daly, but Mum had accepted it.

At the thought of Mum, I realized there was at least one thing I could do. I rang up the hospital and asked how she was. She was fine. Monday or Tuesday they were going to move her to the cottage hospital.

"Tell her I'll ring every night. When the cheap rate starts," I said. "I'm no good at writing and the postbox is miles away." Thank goodness I thought of that. Mum would expect a card at least.

It was only seven o'clock then. I messed about for another half an hour. Tried the telly very softly and peered through the dark living-room window at Mum's bag of nuts hanging on the clothesline. Then I made up my mind that tomorrow I would tell Bruce who my father was and try to sell him the idea of having me in the family. Tomorrow I would phone Dad and try to sell *him* the idea of me as the great negotiator. Dad wouldn't buy it, of course—he'd go mad—but funnily enough I knew I could rely on Daly to understand.

I felt better when I'd sorted that lot out. I hung over Bruce for a bit and felt his forehead. Then I went to bed with the last of the bread and a packet of cream cheese from Mum's store.

The next morning it was Sunday and the street was as quiet as the grave. There was no wind, no rain, no people. We don't get a Sunday milk delivery, so I couldn't sneak out and pinch a bottle off someone's doorstep. I warmed the rest of the soup and got Bruce to drink it, but when I went downstairs and left him in the bathroom I could hear him retching again. I whipped back upstairs and hissed at him through the door not to run the tap into the basin. He didn't reply, so I went in. He was in a little heap on the floor with his head on the loo seat.

"It's all right," he kept saying all the time I carried

him back to bed and sponged his face. "Don't worry, Dave. It's all right."

"Just relax." Mum always told people to relax. "I want to talk something over with you, kiddo, so relax and take it easy."

His arms flailed feebly and I took his thin wrists and held them loosely on the eiderdown. At least he was warm.

"I've *got* to tell you something, Bruce." His eyes were half shut. This was going to be difficult. I pressed on glumly. About that first Saturday at the old Albert Rooms and Dad thinking so much of his new friend. And me being—well—jealous. Hating the woman. Looking for a weapon to use against her. And finding her son.

Bruce's eyes flickered and opened. I couldn't look at him. I tried to explain how my jealousy must have died without me even knowing it. How the last bit must have gone up in a puff of smoke when I realized Bruce and me—we'd be brothers.

"It's okay, Dave . . ." Bruce whispered again. "Don't cry. It's okay. Honest."

He was holding my wrist now. Comforting me. That's good for a laugh, isn't it? A little sick kid like Bruce comforting a hulking great kid like me.

After a bit we were quiet. Just sitting there, looking through the window at the gray December sky. I felt a curious sense of peace. As if I might at last have got hold of what it was all about.

Then Bruce said, "But you do see, Dave. . . . You do see, don't you, why I can't go back?"

I looked back at him. He seemed old.

122

"We'll be able to see more of each other, kiddo. I'll help you—I can carry you easily. We could go to football—like those blokes said last night. Up at the East End."

I sounded strangely like a little kid battering at the wall of adult know-how. He didn't even bother to grin at me.

"When I saw them together . . . Alan and Mum . . . Funny, I never thought he was your Dad, but there was something about him. I liked him. Anyway, I knew . . . like you did, Dave." His voice faded and I leaned closer. "They're right, aren't they? I mean, they really look at each other."

Somehow I nodded. "Yes. Yes . . . I guess they do." I sat up. "It's no good fighting against it. They ought to get married and be together. That's it."

Bruce's thin voice was slightly stronger. "That's what I told her. Mum. I told her that. And she just said what nonsense and I'd been watching too many telly films."

I frowned. Daly had said that?

"She was only *saying* that. She didn't mean it—" I began.

"Course she was. Because of me. Because she doesn't want Alan lumbered with—with—with a—with a—!"

I clapped my hand over his mouth. "Shut up!" I hissed. "My dad thinks you're great! He's told me so. And he's told me how proud your mum is of you. You don't know what you're talking about—"

"She won't marry him, Dave. She told me so. That's why I had to disappear—I knew she'd turn to Alan then—he'd help her and look after her. And it's working. She was outside with him yesterday—they were to-gether—" He was jerking about convulsively on the bed; I could hardly understand him.

"Okay. So it's worked," I said decisively. "I'll phone her and let her know." I tried to sound master of the situation again, but I was just as scared as I'd been last night. And something else. Ashamed. Bruce's motives were so different from mine.

He started bubbling something again. I grabbed a bit of toilet roll I'd put by the bed and wiped his mouth; then I pinioned his arms and flung my leg over him. We sprawled, panting and glaring at each other.

Gradually we both calmed down. Bruce sort of nodded at me and I let him go and sat back on the side of the mattress. The sheets and blankets were in knots all over the place. I tried to tidy up a bit. I suppose that's why nurses are forever making beds; it makes things more normal. Like dishing out cups of tea. Well, I couldn't do that without any milk.

"Sorry." Bruce sounded faint but better.

" 'S okay. . . ." I wandered over to the window and looked out. A few blokes were coming down the road from the pub, so it was gone two. Of course it had taken me a long time to explain to Bruce who I was . . . then we'd just sat still for ages . . . then he'd told me the real reason for his disappearance. But we'd used up the morning and I hadn't telephoned like I meant to.

I turned back to the bed. He was asleep. I stared down at him. Such a little kid, so weak and helpless. Yet he'd done this thing. For his mum.

I was crying again. I turned my back on him and

124

pressed my head hard against the window frame. The thought that had been with me unacknowledged ever since yesterday morning gradually took shape. For me, this whole thing had been a giant escapade to stir things up between Dad and Daly . . . to score off the big adult world. On a par with jumping for the Box Kite in the museum.

For Bruce, it had been something much more permanent. I remembered the desperation in his eyes on Friday afternoon as he came skidding down Church Road. He hadn't been going to stop. He'd been going to go right out into the traffic. Even when I turned up and offered a way out, he'd only taken it as a temporary measure.

Bruce was going to let himself die. He was going— quite deliberately—to give his mum and my dad a clear field.

14

I know what I should have done. Right then. I should have gone to the phone and called the whole thing off. I'd have been okay then. Almost like a rescuer. A ruddy hero. Dad might have looked skeptical, but Daly would have loved me. So would Bartlett, Miss Ruskin, Jess . . . all the people I wanted to think well of me.

But I didn't, did I?

Why didn't I? Was it because I somehow respected

Bruce's decision? I certainly respected him like hell. Maybe that was it. I couldn't let him start out on something so . . . big . . . just to squash it because I was frightened. Then again, maybe I didn't like to admit that the responsibility for Bruce was getting too much for me. Dammit, if he could look out the window and see his mother yesterday morning—see his way back to security and comfort—and keep his trap shut, who was I to throw it all away for him when he was asleep?

So I decided to let him sleep for a while and hope when he woke up I could persuade him to be . . . sensible.

I fiddled round the bedroom checking the fire and the electric blanket and dusting off Mum's dressing table with my elbow; then when Bruce still didn't stir, I went downstairs and opened a tin of meat and a packet of cream crackers and ate the lot. Then I did the bit where I peered through all the windows and walked around thinking about Mum. Then I drank some water and went and looked at Bruce again. He was still asleep.

That went on till six o'clock. Then I put the telly on and was just in time to catch the news flash about Bruce.

It was horrible. Like the bit where Tom Sawyer goes to his own funeral and realizes it isn't funny anymore. There was a picture of Bruce and a film of an interview with Daly. She was very still and controlled. She said if anyone found Bruce would they ring an ambulance immediately as he was on steroids.

I switched off and galloped upstairs. He looked the same. Very small and very still. Was he just going to go on sleeping until he died? I thought back over the last two days. All he'd had to eat was that cheese sandwich soaked in tea, the milk yesterday and about an eggcup of tinned soup.

I turned back the clothes and felt in his jeans pockets. He stirred and murmured something and his errant arm soared up and caught me under the chin. But his eyes didn't open.

In his back pocket there was a card in a plastic envelope. It said, "I am a patient on steroid treatment, which must not be stopped abruptly. . . ." I didn't read further.

"Bruce—Bruce, wake up!" I shook him, not very gently. Panic was making my heart jump about like it had when Dad rolled up yesterday. "Bruce!"

His eyes opened slowly. Then—thank God—he smiled. He looked for a moment like the old Bruce at Underwood. Cheerful, eternally optimistic.

I said roughly, "What's this about steroid treatment?" I waved the card under his nose.

"Oh, that . . ." His voice was thick with sleep. "My tablets. Build me up. Case I get any infection . . ." His smile deepened into a grin as if that was some kind of big joke.

I remembered that long, ice-cold trek from Bristol, the lack of nourishment. . . . "Look, Bruce. You've got to eat something. Seriously. You must try."

His head went from side to side on the pillow, slowly and wearily.

"We've been into all that, Dave. Thought you understood."

It had to be said. I'd got to say it.

My voice wavered from bass to treble. "You're not going to die, Bruce. Get that? I'm not going to let you die."

He went on grinning.

I said desperately, "Bruce! D'you want to make me a murderer? You've got to eat something—otherwise I get straight on the phone to your mother—"

"No." His head went again. "Not after all this, Dave. You can't." I must have looked determined, because he stopped smiling and sighed. "Okay. Warm some milk and sugar. That's what I have. . . ." His eyelids drooped. "I'm tired, Dave. But I'm okay. Honest. I won't let you down. . . ."

I frowned down at him. Was he putting it on? He sounded all right—tired like he said, but all right. And he'd kept that milk down yesterday. The only trouble was, we'd got no more.

After a bit I got up and went downstairs again. I didn't know what to do. I picked up the phone, but in the end I just dialed the hospital and asked how Mum was. The Sister said she was doing fine and was waiting to speak to me and would I hang on.

Then Mum's voice. "Dave? Hello, love. How's it going?"

"Fine . . ." I didn't want to be pushed into any lies. "The weather's fine. But we're staying indoors most of the time. How about you?"

"Marvelous. Looking forward to going into the cottage hospital on Tuesday. Your friend Jess came in this afternoon with a lovely box of chocolates. Wasn't it good of her?"

"Yeah." Good old Jess. Jess. Hang on a minute. She'd help out with Bruce.

"You sound so near, Dave."

"Yeah. So do you. I'll have to go, Mum. I'll try and ring again tomorrow."

"Listen. Wait a minute. I must tell you. Dad came in to see me yesterday. Mrs. Firbright told him about the operation, but it wasn't that. . . . Dave—are you there?"

"Yes, Mum." My heart was going again.

"Now don't let it spoil your holiday or anything. He came to tell me about a boy you know at that special school—"

I swallowed something. "Bruce?"

"That's it. Bruce Daly. He's missing—disappeared from the school or something. Dad seemed to think you might know where he could have gone. Apparently this boy—Bruce—thinks a lot of you, Dave."

"I heard about it. On the telly."

"Oh." Mum sounded doubtful and I remembered describing the cottage as Stone Age. "Oh, we didn't think you'd know. . . . Anyway, love, Dad was talking about coming to see you. He was going to Harkins' place to get some directions. So don't be surprised if he rolls up."

I felt like spewing up. "Thanks for letting me know, Mum. I must go. Tomorrow, okay?"

"Take care of yourself, love. Don't stay in wet clothes, whatever you do."

"Okay, Mum. Cheerio."

"Good-bye, love."

I put the receiver down and stared at the wallpaper.

This was how a fox must feel with the hounds at the mouth of his earth.

Suddenly the phone started to ring and I nearly hit the roof. The noise was appalling, like a fire alarm. I knew I couldn't answer it, but in my frightened condition I imagined it would bring Mrs. Firbright round hotfoot. She'd think it was a marvelous excuse to break a window and get in for a good old nosey. And it was Dad. I knew it was Dad.

I was stuck there, paralyzed, for a second. Then I tore into the living room and grabbed a cushion and held it tightly over the whole telephone. The sound became blessedly muffled. It went on for about a dozen rings, then stopped. In the silence I heard a voice muttering, "Shut up, please shut up. . . ." It was me.

How long I crouched over that cushion I don't know, but at last I sort of collapsed onto the hall floor and picked up the directory. It didn't do me much good to see my finger was trembling as I ran down the H's looking for Henshawe. Of course Jess wasn't there. Didn't she live with her grandparents or something? I shut the book and sat there gripping it hard, trying to think what to do.

Supposing the worst had happened and Dad had gone to Devon and found out I wasn't there. He still didn't know where I was. Ma Firbright was the best witness he could have to that. Still . . . he would come here, because there would be nowhere else to try. And even if I didn't answer the door, he'd break in and search the place. And I couldn't move out with Bruce like he was.

I suddenly found I wasn't gripping the book anymore. I was sort of relaxing, slumping against the hall wall.

130

Yes, it would be a relief to see Dad. Dad would take it all out of my hands. I'd rather Dad than anyone. The alternatives were the Firbrights or some other nosey neighbors—or the police.

I looked at my watch. Just coming up to seven. Dad would have phoned immediately he found out I wasn't with Buff. So now he'd be starting back. Four hours at the outside. More likely three. Only three more hours.

I stood up. I felt better. Somehow Dad would get us out of any trouble with the police and Bruce would be all right, and we'd be back to where we were. Meanwhile . . . I was going to get some milk for Bruce.

I went upstairs and told him what I was going to do, but I don't know whether he understood. He looked pretty awful. I felt a tinge of anxiety in case Dad was delayed on the road or decided to put off his call till tomorrow.

I went back down double quick and wedged the cushion over the phone with a couple of Wonderlands of Knowledge; then I switched off all the lights and unlocked the kitchen door as if the key was made of glass. I opened the door a crack and stood there listening. Faint music from Firbrights', distant cars; no footsteps. I locked the door behind me and sneaked down the side path and ran up the road at a jog trot.

Not one house in our road had left Saturday's milk out.

Cursing under my breath, I turned down Chapel Lane and did both sides of that. Nothing. I slowed down indecisively. I could go on all night like this. I tried to think where there might be a milk machine, or a cafe

131

open. Our town is described in the guidebook as a "charming Victorian backwater." We didn't have milk machines or all-night cafes.

I kept going hopelessly. I suppose it was natural to make for the chip shop, a kind of homing instinct. Anyway I did, and there under the awning outside the shuttered shop Jasper was standing, as usual, kicking a stone in the gutter and waiting for the girls from the convent to come out of Vespers or wherever they went on Sunday nights.

He stood stock-still when he saw me, his mouth sort of sagging.

"That you, Wint? What the hell—?"

"Course it's me." Why hadn't I thought of old Jasper before? I didn't know where Jess lived, and in any case, I didn't want to drop her into any of this trouble. But Jasper was born to trouble. "Gosh, am I glad to see you," I finished, like a kid spotting Father Christmas.

"You are?" He looked astonished. Of course, the last time we'd met had been in the bike sheds after the Gilbert and Sullivan thing. Seemed years ago. "Look, Wint. What you doing here? I thought— I mean, if I'd realized that swine wasn't taking you along either, I wouldn't have organized anything—"

"Forget it, Jas. I was going with Buff and we both deserved what we got. Okay? Forget it."

"Yeah. Sure. But listen. What you doing here?" He sounded like a cracked record.

"I didn't go, did I? Jas—I need some milk. Can you get some for me?"

"*Milk?*" He looked incredulous. "What the hell you on about? Milk?"

132

"Pay attention, Jas. I've got to have some milk for a friend of mine. He's sick and he can't take normal food. I don't want anyone to know about him—or me, for that matter. Can you fix it?"

There was a little pause. A couple of the convent girls went by and we ignored them. I could almost hear Jasper's brain ticking.

He said slowly, "The spastic kid. It was on telly. And you and Jess Henshawe visit them, don't you? For your environmental thing. Christ . . . you've kidnapped him, Wint."

It was a bit of a shock, him using that word. I tried to brush it off. "Bloody nonsense. I'm not *really* Bogart, y'know, Jas. I'm just such a good actor."

"You've got him, though, haven't you? Down at your place? Course, your Mum's in hospital or something. Christ, Wint. You've gone too far this time."

I got hold of his duffel and shook him hard.

"Listen, Jas. Snap out of it, will you? Bruce has been hiding out with me, fair enough. My dad's coming to collect him tonight, but he's nearly passing out because he can't take anything except milk. Now . . ." I spoke slowly, right into his face. "Can you get me . . . one bottle . . . of milk?"

"Sure—sure, Wint." He jerked free. "I get the message. It's just a bit of a shock seeing you here when you should be with Buff. And you—doing this—when you've been Jackie Ruskin's pet since half term."

"Oh, come on, Jas. I'm no one's pet. And I haven't done anything so awful. This kid . . . he's nice, you'd like him. And he had a bit of a rough deal. So he dropped out for a couple of days."

"Sure. Sure, Wint. I believe you. You don't have to convince *me*. Okay?" He started to grin. "You got Jess Henshawe down there, too, kiddo?"

If I hadn't wanted that milk so bad, I'd have hit him then. But I did want the milk.

"Shut your face, Jas. You've got a mind like a sewer. Are you going to get me some milk or not?"

"Sure. Sure, Wint. Come on. Let's go."

He lived about ten minute's walk from the chip shop. During that short time, he got most of the story out of me except for the vital bit about Dad and Bruce's mum. So it probably did sound as if I was doing the whole thing for the hell of it. He kept assuring me I was doing great, man. Just great.

Anyway, he sneaked a pint of milk out to me, and I thanked him. I didn't swear him to secrecy or anything like that. Jas and me had never split on each other.

I legged it back home and got in without seeing a soul. That's the best of living in a charming Victorian backwater. It's dead on a Sunday night.

Milk in saucepan, add sugar, swill it round over the gas to stop it catching. Into mug. Upstairs again.

Bruce was still sleeping, but he woke at my first touch and smiled immediately.

"Telephone rang," he whispered. "I could only just hear it."

"I muffled it with a cushion. Here, drink this. Come on, sit up. I'll hold it." He drank slowly, slurping a lot down his chin. I mopped as best I could. We rested and tried again. After about ten minutes he'd had nearly half a pint. I wanted to cheer. It seemed to me he looked fatter already.

134

"Well done, kiddo. You can have the other half later. When we know that lot's going to stay down."

"Okay. I wish you wouldn't worry, Dave. There's nothing to worry about."

I said soberly, "Did you really think I could let you . . . go . . . like that?"

He made an upside-down grin, ashamed. "I suppose not. You always seem so cheerful. . . . I don't know."

"That doesn't mean anything. Me being cheerful."

He lay back weakly for a bit. Then he said, "You going to ring my mum tomorrow?"

"I don't need to, Bruce. Sorry, but they're onto us. That was Dad on the phone. He'll probably be here about ten o'clock."

"Oh." He didn't sound surprised. "What's the time now, Dave?"

"Eight-fifteen. . . . You're not too bothered, are you, kiddo?"

"I suppose not. Was it all a waste of time, Dave?"

"No. They'll get together now."

"But I'll be . . . there. I'm sorry, Dave, but I hate it."

"You can be with us a lot of the time. Mum and me. She's a nurse. And anyway, I can look after you."

"But . . . I'm no *good*, Dave. Can't you see?"

"You make me sick. No good." I mimicked his voice. "What good is anyone, come to that? You make people nicer than they were before, Bruce."

"Who, for instance?"

"Me, for instance!"

I was still glaring at him when the door knocker cracked like thunder through the house.

I didn't even bother to look out of the window, so certain was I that it was Dad. I made a wry face at Bruce and said something about it being okay; then I took the stairs in three bounds and unbolted the front door.

Two policemen stood on the doorstep. Behind them, their patrol car relaying information and a sleek black car was drawing up behind it and disgorging plain-clothes types.

Jasper stood near the gate. His eyes didn't meet mine.

15

So I didn't turn out to be a hero after all, did I? A lot of people still remember the publicity, so I need not go into all that. It was pretty awful. Especially that interview on telly when the man kept asking me what I would have done if Bruce had died. Then there were those articles in the paper about the amoral attitude of our teenagers. I thought amoral meant the same as immoral and I didn't get it for ages. When Mum told me it was sort of irresponsible, it got me. I mean, all along—the whole darned time—I'd tried to think out what I was doing.

Anyway, it got so I couldn't go out or anything without some smart aleck wanting to talk to me. I spent Christmas at Gran's and just got through it before they tracked me down. Then the Harkinses turned up trumps and offered Mum and me the cottage in North Devon until the end of January. Dad took us down and stayed a couple of nights. We were happy in a very quiet sort of way.

I think the thing that really stuck in me after all the fuss died down was Jasper. All right, so he was a bad boy, he could cheat in exams, lie his way out of anything, pick fights and even do a bit of shoplifting in the supermarket. But we were mates. We'd shared so many tedious hours together in the classroom and outside the chip shop. Okay, we'd had that fight in the bike sheds. That was nothing. When I looked past those two coppers and saw Jasper at our front gate, I really felt the world was collapsing.

I suppose he thought I was the rat. Yes, looking at it from his point of view, I guess that's what he must have thought. I'd stopped meeting him after school. I'd started taking an interest in something *at* school. I spent time with Buff and with Jess. Somehow I wangled an invitation to Devon and he didn't. And then I made the final scoop without him. . . . I kidnapped someone.

I wonder what kind of revenge he thought he was taking when he went to the cop shop that night? Did he really see me behind bars or in a reformatory? It might have happened. Yes, it could have happened if Margaret Daly had been a different sort of woman.

But she wasn't. There were no "proceedings." I escaped that at least. Not that I'd have cared much, but Mum would. So would Dad. When Dad turned up that night—only half an hour after the police—I began to understand that his feeling for Bruce's mum didn't change anything he felt for me. Or maybe for Mum. I don't know. . . . He was marvelous that night. He sorted out the muddle and the misunderstandings. By ten o'clock, Bruce and me were tucked up in bed and he'd fetched Bruce's mum, and all she said was "Thank you, David. I couldn't have looked after him better myself." I started to cry at that—I did a hell of a lot of crying that weekend, didn't I?—but the police sergeant had said some pretty nasty things before she turned up. Dad sort of hugged me against his arm then, and Daly said, "Don't worry about them, David. You saved Bruce's life. That's all I know."

Of course it wasn't quite like that. Margaret Daly had her son back and that was all she cared about. Mum and Dad knew differently . . . but then again, they thought a lot of me.

It was people like Bartlett, Miss Ruskin . . . Jess. It wouldn't take them long to understand my real motives. To feel I was a rat. Like I thought Jasper was a rat.

Miss Ruskin came to see me at Gran's after that telly interview. We were together for nearly an hour, but we didn't talk much. I tried to explain, and she said I didn't have to tell her anything because she hadn't come to judge me, just to pay a call like any other friend. Gran brought us in some tea and mince pies, and Miss Ruskin told us she was leaving school to do social work for the Council. Unmarried mothers or something.

When she got up to go, she said, "David. Try to write it all down. It's part of your environmental study, so you should make a report in any case. But put it all down. Your feelings. Everything. When you read it, you might discover something."

138

So I have. I sent a copy to Bartlett like I promised, and he wrote and asked me to go on visiting Underwood now I understood what it was all about.

And I sent a copy to Jess and she wrote, too. Her spelling was still up the creek, but I got the message. She wanted me to go to the Railway Exhibition with her and her grandfather when I got back from Devon. Perhaps that was what it was all about . . . Jess and me?

It's all people, though. Not just Jess. Mum. Dad. Daly. Doc Mathieson. Jasper and Buff and Mart—even Rorie. Miss Ruskin and the Games bloke—Eccles. Those women in the hospital with Mum . . . one of them died and Mum cried her eyes out. The people at Underwood, kids and teachers.

And Bruce. Through it all, there was Bruce.

Bruce and me . . . we will be brothers. Soon, I expect. And Mum thinks the world of Bruce, so he'll be staying at our place quite a lot.

Yes. There ought to be a nice clear meaning to it all, oughtn't there? But I still don't really know what it's all about.

The only thing is, when Miss Ruskin first asked that question in her room that November afternoon when I'd skipped rugby, I thought there was no answer—just a raspberry, maybe. I thought there was nothing for it to be about, if you get me.

Now . . . well, now at least I know it's all about *something*.

Perhaps that's all Miss Ruskin wanted me to discover anyway?

Format by Gloria Bressler
Set in 11 pt. Times Roman
Composed, printed and bound by Vail-Ballou Press, Inc.
HARPER & ROW, PUBLISHERS, INCORPORATED